W·I·T·C·H

Will   Irma   Taranee   Cornelia   Hay Lin

Farewell to Love

Adapted by ALICE ALFONSI

WITHDRAWN

HYPERION PAPERBACKS FOR CHILDREN
New York

© 2007 Disney Enterprises, Inc.

W.I.T.C.H. Will Irma Taranee Cornelia Hay Lin is a trademark of Disney Enterprises, Inc. Hyperion Paperbacks for Children is an imprint of Disney Children's Book Group, L.L.C.

Printed in the United States of America
First Edition
1 3 5 7 9 10 8 6 4 2

This book is set in 12/16.5 Hiroshige Book.
ISBN 1-4231-0267-3
Visit www.clubwitch.com

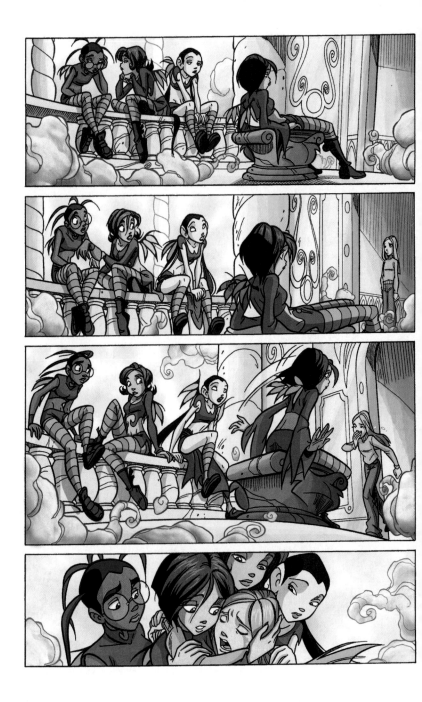

ONE

With powerful strides, Caleb's long legs swept him through the endless halls of the Temple. There were hundreds of rooms in the majestic structure—not to mention thousands of sites for meditation. Caleb was determined to search every one.

For far too long, the young warrior had felt like a trapped animal in this spiritual dimension. The Elders who populated Candracar were always cool, calm, and quiet. They were all about thought. Caleb, on the other hand, was a warrior. He was all about action.

Of course, Caleb was the one who'd gotten himself there in the first place. When he'd pledged his service to the Oracle, he'd locked himself inside his own ethereal cage. Now that cage door stood open, and he was anxious to flee.

But first he had to find the Oracle, no easy feat in a place as enormous as the Temple of Candracar!

Caleb propelled himself determinedly through the maze of ornate hallways. Before long, he felt the presence of an energy field. The sensation was faint at first. But as he followed it, the force grew stronger. It drew him toward the Lotus Room.

Stepping through an arched doorway, he entered a chamber so huge it took his breath away. This one room was taller than ten cathedrals in Metamoor put together. A wide, blue pool took up most of the space inside it. Pink and violet lotus flowers bobbed in the shimmering water, while fat clouds drifted in lazy circles near the ceiling.

Craning his neck, Caleb shaded his eyes from the brilliant light streaming in through the transparent roof. A small figure knelt on a floating platform high above, among the clouds. Even from that distance, Caleb could feel the intensity of the being's aura.

"I'm ready, Oracle!" Caleb called. His loud

voice wavered slightly as he gazed up at the floating figure.

For some time now, Caleb had served the Oracle, yet he still felt intimidated in the seer's presence. Who wouldn't be? he thought. After all, the Oracle watched over billions of life-forms throughout the universe. No one really knew the depths of his power, not even there in Candracar, the center of infinity. But one thing Caleb did know was that that tiny benevolent being was the only one who had the authority to say whether he, Caleb, could stay or go.

For a long, silent moment, the Oracle failed to react to Caleb's arrival. He remained in meditation, hands clasped, eyes closed. Finally, his eyelids fluttered open, and his penetrating gaze focused on the young man standing below him.

"If you are ready," the Oracle said softly, "then come with me to the hall of the Congregation. The Elders of Candracar would like to say good-bye to you."

Caleb's tense limbs relaxed.

It's really happening, he thought. At last, I can go home!

As Caleb watched, the Oracle's platform descended. Stepping off its smooth golden surface, he walked across the crystal bridge. Caleb took his place behind him. Together they moved out of the bright Lotus Room and into the cool shadows of the Temple hallway.

Quietly, the Oracle padded through the network of corridors, each one decorated with symbols and artwork from hundreds of different worlds. Caleb expected their entire walk to be silent. But the Oracle surprised him with a sudden question.

"Cornelia didn't understand your decision, did she?"

Caleb swallowed uneasily. He knew the answer to that question. It was no. Cornelia didn't understand. She had cried and run away from him. She'd been hurt, confused, and angry.

But the last thing Caleb wanted to do was dwell on Cornelia's heartache. He still cared deeply for her. And it hurt him to see her so upset about their parting. Still . . . more than anything, Caleb wished to see his home again. Cornelia's tears weren't going to change that wish.

"Time heals all," he told the Oracle.

Caleb believed it, too. After all, Cornelia

was a Guardian. She had amazing strength of spirit. He believed she would get over him, and her heartache, in time.

The Oracle lifted a skeptical eyebrow. "Time can't always succeed where we fail," he warned. "Occasionally time is entrusted with tasks that are too demanding."

"Oracle, it was a difficult decision," Caleb said defensively, "and—"

The Oracle lifted a hand and smiled. "Oh, don't take that as personal criticism, Caleb. What I said goes for me, as well."

Caleb blinked in shock. He had never heard the Oracle admit that even he, the most powerful being in Candracar, could actually make mistakes.

It was hard to deny those mistakes, though, when one considered that the Oracle's actions—or, rather, inaction—had nearly allowed the deranged sorceress, Nerissa, to destroy Candracar.

And what's more, the Oracle's decisions would not have affected just him. If Candracar had fallen, then the worlds it watched over would have fallen, too. Maybe not right away, but in time, Nerissa's evil magic would have spread to the rest of the universe and poisoned other civilizations.

Earth would have been one of the first worlds to go, which is one reason the five Guardians had fought so very hard to destroy Nerissa and save Candracar. Beneath their dazzling winged forms, their striped leggings and long, strong limbs, Will, Irma, Taranee, Cornelia, and Hay Lin were really young human girls from Heatherfield, a small town on earth.

In their own world, the Guardians went to school, had families, and lived normal, human lives.

However, when Caleb had first met Cornelia and her friends, they'd been in their glittering Guardian forms far from earth. So Caleb had assumed they were supernatural beings.

He wasn't exactly wrong. While they were human, each girl had special abilities. Cornelia was able to manipulate earth; Irma, water; Taranee, fire; and Hay Lin, air. Individually, their talents were strong, but together the girls were a mighty force. It was Will, their leader, who carried the power to unite them. She was the Keeper of the Heart of Candracar. The

Heart was an ancient, mystical crystal that magnified and united the girls' powers, which they used to protect the earth and the entire universe from evil . . . including Caleb's own world of Metamoor.

For that, Caleb would always be grateful.

Not long ago, Metamoor had been under the rule of a vicious prince named Phobos. For years, Phobos had terrorized the people of Metamoor. He'd robbed them of everything with his dark magic: their crops, their goods, and their way of life.

If Phobos suspected any citizens of being his enemy, he sent soldiers to arrest them. And Phobos's dungeon was one of the darkest, cruelest pits in the universe.

From the Temple of Candracar, the Oracle watched the growing suffering and chaos on Metamoor. He created a magical Veil around the world to keep Phobos's evil isolated from the rest of the universe. But eventually the magic of the Veil began to weaken at certain points, creating portals of escape.

Evil was threatening to spread to the earth and beyond, so the Oracle anointed a new generation of Guardians. He'd allowed Yan Lin, a former Guardian herself and Hay Lin's grandmother, to initiate the girls and pass on to them their means of transformation—the Heart of Candracar.

Calling themselves W.I.T.C.H., a name they had created from their own initials, the girls were assigned their first mission: to close the portals between the earth and Metamoor. Then they focused on defeating Prince Phobos, the source of all things evil in Metamoor.

Caleb himself had been fighting Phobos for years. He was a Murmurer, a flowerlike creature created by Phobos to spy on the people of Meridian. But unlike many of his kind, he rebelled against Phobos's rule.

Something inside him resisted serving evil. Something inside him decided to fight back. He managed to break free of his flowerlike form and joined the rebellion against Phobos. Soon he became a rebel leader.

Living the life of a fugitive wasn't easy. Caleb often went hungry. He felt the sting of battle wounds. And he witnessed the arrest of many good friends. But the more Caleb fought for others, the stronger his drive became. And finally, after a long fight, the rebels won.

After W.I.T.C.H. helped the rebels defeat Phobos, the prince's younger sister, Elyon, took the throne. For years, Elyon had been living in Heatherfield, unaware that her true identity was that of heir to the Meridian throne, or that she even had a brother.

Years before, two rebels from Meridian had brought Elyon to Heatherfield; they had feared for her life amid the turmoil in Metamoor and wanted to make sure that she, the true Light of Meridian, remained safe from Phobos. Elyon was brought up as a normal girl on earth. No one was more surprised than she to discover that her destiny was to rule a foreign land. After the battle with Phobos ended, the Light of Meridian returned. Metamoor and its capital city were once again free, and they flourished under their rightful ruler—Elyon.

For Caleb, however, the prince's defeat was bittersweet. Before he was unseated, Phobos had cast a spell that returned Caleb to his original flower form.

Cornelia was heartbroken. By that point, she had fallen in love with Caleb, and she was devastated at the prospect of never being able to speak to him again. She took him in his flower form back to Heatherfield, where she nursed him and kept him alive.

Cornelia loved Caleb so much that she violated the laws of Candracar and used all five Guardian powers to transform him back into the almost human form she knew and loved. The only remaining signs of Caleb's previous form were the bright green stripes on his cheeks.

Unfortunately, when Cornelia helped Caleb, she had broken Candracar's rules. And the Oracle and Elders were obligated to punish her for her actions.

Caleb couldn't allow that to happen. He boldly stepped up to protect Cornelia, offering his services for the rest of his life to the Oracle. The only thing he asked in return was that Cornelia remain free of punishment.

The Oracle accepted Caleb's offer and appointed him the Herald of Candracar.

Then the terrible sorceress Nerissa escaped from her prison. Using the darkest powers in existence, she attacked Caleb and the Guardians.

Caleb was badly hurt. It took time for him to

heal. But once he did, he stepped up again—this time to defend Nerissa's final target, Candracar.

The battle against Nerissa had been tough, but Caleb had fought courageously, and for that, the Oracle was now releasing him from his service. Caleb was finally free. Unfortunately, that freedom also meant he had another choice to make. A choice that would affect both him *and* Cornelia.

He would always love Cornelia. But he knew that their life together was not meant to be. Beneath her turquoise wings and glittering Guardian facade was a young human girl with a tender heart and a separate destiny.

For her own good, Caleb had to let her go. Sure, some part of him wished she could come to Metamoor with him. But Cornelia's life was back in Heatherfield. She had a family. She attended school.

Caleb, however, knew Cornelia wouldn't understand. She wanted him to go back to Heatherfield with her. But he could never do that!

He wouldn't have fit in at Sheffield Institute.

He would have been living a lie, never revealing his true self. And Caleb was proud of what he was—a warrior from Metamoor, a rebel with strong convictions.

I've spent enough time away from my home, he thought. I cannot keep denying what I am. To constrict who you really are just to fit into someone else's world . . . it's too much to ask! Even in the name of love.

"I heard that you won't be alone during your return," the Oracle said, causing Caleb to return to the present. "You'll be taking the nurse Galgheita with you."

Caleb smiled as he followed the Oracle. "It's strange to hear her real name again."

The Oracle nodded. "For a long time, in order to protect Elyon, she lived far from Metamoor, as the human called Mrs. Rudolph. I hope that your people will give her the welcome she deserves."

"I'm certain that her loyalty and sacrifices will be given the highest of honors," Caleb replied.

The Oracle moved into the Great Hall, an enormous arena with a gallery of seats spiraling up from the mist-shrouded floor. Hundreds of

Elders were watching from the balconies.

Some of the Elders were human, but many were not. Their faces and forms were all quite different. Their skin, scales, horns, and fur were all of different colors and textures. But whether they had ears or antennae, snouts or noses, all the Elders there were equal. All had come from the many worlds that Candracar watched over and protected.

In the center of the hall stood a golden pedestal. A tall, robed man waited at the top. His white hair and beard were long and flowing, and his wrinkles looked older than time itself.

This was Tibor, the Oracle's faithful adviser.

The Oracle climbed the steps to join him at the top of the pedestal. Then he sank to his knees, clasped his hands together, and pulled them inside his robe's wide, bell-like sleeves. Finally, he turned to address Caleb again.

"And what about you, Caleb?" he asked.

Caleb's big brown eyes widened. "Me?" He had followed the Oracle to the top of the platform and now stood beside him.

The Oracle smiled. "Are you ready to be given a hero's welcome?"

Caleb humbly shook his head of shaggy brown hair. "It would be an unmerited privilege, Oracle," he said.

And he meant it, too. Caleb wasn't going back to Metamoor for praise. He was going back because it was his home, because he missed his friends, and because he knew it was where he belonged.

Just then, Caleb saw five beautiful young women approaching the pedestal. The fiery redhead was Will, the leader of the Guardians. The slender one with blue-black pigtails was Hay Lin. The one with the large, round glasses and the cool, thoughtful look was Taranee. The brown-haired, smirking one was Irma. And last but far from least was Cornelia, the stunning blond Guardian, whom Caleb *still* loved deeply.

"Guardians, I'm entrusting Caleb to you," the Oracle announced. "He is no longer the Herald of Candracar and is once again a free being. You will accompany him to Meridian on his last journey."

Irma folded her arms and glared at Caleb. "Today," she muttered, "I'd rather accompany a truckload of skunks."

The Oracle ignored the outspoken water

Guardian and cleared his throat. "Does anyone have an objection to make?"

"I do, sir!" The shaky voice was Cornelia's.

Caleb's fists were clenched so tightly his knuckles blanched. He could see that Cornelia's lovely blue eyes were watery and swollen. Her face was streaked with dried tears. The signs of her heartache stabbed his heart, but Caleb said nothing. He was a warrior. He'd suffered many wounds in battle. If there was one thing he knew how to do, it was to endure pain silently.

The Oracle nodded at Cornelia, and she approached his golden pedestal. Even though Caleb stood right beside the Oracle, Cornelia carefully avoided looking at the boy she loved. Instead, the earth Guardian kept her focus exclusively on the small, serene Oracle.

"I'd like to be excused from this task," she said. Her voice started out shaky but gradually grew stronger. "My friends will do just fine without me."

The Oracle said nothing; then Cornelia made a suggestion. "I'd be happy to go back to Heatherfield to help Mrs. Rudolph."

Tibor's bushy eyebrows came together like

woolly white caterpillars. "This is an unusual request," he said. "Guardians always travel together as a group."

"I know, Tibor," the Oracle told his adviser, "but that is a rule for which we can make an exception." The Oracle glanced at Caleb, then returned his gaze to the young Guardian. "Your wish is granted, Cornelia."

As Cornelia turned to rejoin her friends, Caleb also stepped down from the Oracle's platform. He suddenly felt uneasy about the situation. He'd never considered how the rest of the Guardians would feel about his breakup with Cornelia.

"Maybe I owe you girls an explanation," he said to the other Guardians.

Cornelia spun around. A mixture of fury and pain glittered in her blue eyes. "There's no need, Caleb," she snapped. "We've already figured it all out!"

Caleb frowned. Will, Irma, Hay Lin, and Taranee were all glaring at him. "You guys *are* mad at me, aren't you?"

"Why bother asking?" Irma was clearly not holding back her feelings. "If it was up to me, I'd kick you all the way back to Meridian!"

Caleb ran a hand through his hair. The Guardians were looking at him as if he were some kind of criminal. But as far as he could tell, the only "crime" he'd committed was caring about Cornelia's feelings.

Will walked up to him. Caleb could see she wasn't quite as angry as Irma was, although he doubted she'd be throwing him a going-away party.

"I hope you really understand what you've done," Will said softly, "and that you won't find yourself regretting it one day."

Caleb didn't know what the future held. All he could do was live his life one day at a time, one choice at a time. With a sigh, he met the gaze of the Keeper of the Heart.

"I hope so too, Will," he told her. "I hope so, too."

TWO

Don't freak, Will told herself. *Do. Not. Freak!*

As the Keeper of the Heart and leader of the Guardians, Will wanted to set an example. She knew it would be totally immature to start yelling and ranting at Caleb. Cornelia was trying to hold it together, and Will was following her lead. Yelling at Caleb would probably just embarrass Cornelia more.

But Will found it nearly impossible to hold back her temper. Her best friend was hurting. And Will saw no good reason for her pain.

How could he do it? Will wondered. How could Caleb be so heartless? After everything Cornelia had done for him, after she'd loved him and sacrificed for him, after she'd waited and waited for him, how could Caleb turn around and act like such a dog?

Will noticed that the Oracle was staring intently at her from his golden pedestal. She knew he could sense her anger at Caleb. But then, who wouldn't have? she thought. It certainly didn't take supernatural powers to see that she was totally ticked off!

The Oracle stopped looking at Will, turning for a moment to focus on Caleb. Then he met Will's eyes again. "I, too, have tried to search his soul," he told her, "but it was written that this was how it would end."

Will couldn't believe her ears. "What?" she cried, staring at the small robed being. "Are you saying you knew? You knew what was going to happen between Caleb and Cornelia?"

"Who can say they truly know?" the Oracle replied, in the same soft tone he always used. "I watch, I listen, I reflect, and—"

As the Oracle's words sank in, Will clenched her fists, her entire body shaking with rage.

Don't lose it, Will, warned a tiny voice inside her. *Not in front of the Oracle.* But Will was in no mood to be directed by her little inner voice.

It was way past time she used her real one!

"We're sick and tired of being treated like this!" Will exploded. "We've had enough of doing things your way!"

"Guardian!" The warning bellow came from Tibor, standing by the Oracle's side. The old adviser appeared outraged by Will's outburst. He moved forward to stop her advance up the steps of the pedestal.

But then the Oracle stepped in front of his adviser, holding his palm high. "No, Tibor! Let her air the grievances that have built up in her heart!"

Tibor held his tongue, but he didn't look happy. He stood frowning at Will as the Oracle turned to face her again.

"What is the problem, Will?" the Oracle quietly asked.

"With all due respect, sir," she cried, opening her fists to point at him, "you are the problem!"

A shocked gasp rose from the gallery of the Great Hall as thousands of Elders reacted to Will's outburst. Countless pairs of critical eyes were looking at her now, waiting for her to take back her words, to apologize and slink away.

For a fleeting moment, Will actually felt unsure of herself. But then she glanced over her shoulder and saw that her best friends had stepped closer to her.

Irma was glaring at the Oracle, with her hands on her hips. Hay Lin had folded her arms. Cornelia's hands became shaking fists. And behind her glasses, Taranee's eyes were spitting fire.

Whoa, Will thought. My friends really do have my back!

With renewed courage, she faced the Oracle again.

I've kept my mouth shut long enough, she thought. A true leader must speak out for what's right.

"My friends and I are tired of being treated like pawns in your plans!" Will declared. "The truth has been kept hidden from us far too often. We're happy to serve Candracar, and we're proud of our powers—"

"But we demand to be treated like adults!" Hay Lin shouted.

Will nodded with pride. "Way to go, Hay Lin!"

But not everyone in the hall was proud of

the air Guardian. "Hay Lin!" cried a wrinkled old woman with long gray hair and a brilliant white robe.

"Sorry, Grandma," Hay Lin told the old woman with a sheepish shrug. "That just slipped out!"

Of course, Will knew why Yan Lin was so upset by Hay Lin's outburst. Before she became an Elder in the Congregation, Hay Lin's grandmother had also served as a Guardian, and she had seen firsthand the consequences of scolding the Oracle.

The all-knowing seer might have appeared small and serene, soft-spoken and benevolent, but he was no pushover when it came to confrontations. His response to perceived insubordination was often devastating. Those who dared to criticize his judgment were subject to harsh punishments.

Two of Yan Lin's fellow Guardians had felt the sting of those punishments. They had done the same thing Will and Hay Lin were doing now—openly berating the Oracle, questioning his decisions. The Oracle's response then had been to strip the two of their Guardian status and forever banish them from Candracar.

Will was well aware of the consequences of challenging the Oracle. But she didn't regret her decision. For far too long, the seer had acted just the way Caleb was acting now—totally aloof and arbitrary in his decisions. But those decisions had had a tremendous impact on her and her best friends. And Will was sick and tired of living at the Oracle's whim.

After all, the Guardians had just risked their lives to defend Candracar. They'd fought valiantly against Nerissa's relentless, horrifying attacks—and they'd won. They had saved Candracar and every world it watched over. But when you got right down to it, thought Will, the Oracle was partly responsible for Nerissa's breaking free of her eternal prison in the first place!

Will had never thought of herself as a leader or as particularly courageous. She still remembered that day in Hay Lin's kitchen, when Yan Lin walked in and told them all the truth about the universe: how Candracar watched over thousands of worlds and enlisted Guardians to keep evil from spreading and destroying all that was good.

At first, Will, Irma, Taranee, Cornelia, and

Hay Lin had been totally freaked to hear that they were the new Guardians. Will herself had never thought she'd have the power to fight evil and defend good.

And she certainly had never thought she could tell the most important being in the universe that he was acting like a total jerk!

But Will was full of surprises. She wasn't backing down without a fight.

It's unforgivable, she thought. W.I.T.C.H. saves the universe from a supernasty sorcerer, and this is the thanks we get? Watching our best friend's heart get broken and then listening to the Oracle claim he knew it was going to happen all along?

For the first time, Will really understood why Yan Lin's fellow Guardians, Kadma and Halinor, had become angry enough with the Oracle to risk banishment forever.

But suddenly, a small part of Will, the part of her that actually considered consequences, wondered if this outburst were really worth it. What if the Oracle fired her? she wondered. What if he decided to break up the Guardians and banish them all from Candracar? They would be as lost and forlorn as Kadma and

Halinor, divorced forever from their true destinies. Would they forever regret the day they had spoken out?

Will held her breath, waiting for the worst.

Tibor's expression was one of pure fury. He stepped forward to address the Oracle.

"Sir—" he began.

But the Oracle shook his smooth, hairless head and turned away from the adviser. "Everything's all right, Tibor," he said softly. "I'm going to my chambers. I'm very tired."

Will's jaw dropped. The Oracle wasn't angry at all. If anything, he seemed slightly amused. With a little smile tugging at the corners of his mouth, he glanced back at Will. She could feel the intense power emanating from him. His eyes suddenly seemed as deep as a bottomless well, yet as bright as the Heart that lived inside Will.

"My respects, Guardians," he said.

Then his smile widened, and Will sensed a note of pride in his expression. A fleeting feeling of warmth suddenly suffused her body, as if someone were giving her a heartfelt hug, and Will knew she had done the right thing.

"Sleep well, Oracle," she called as he glided out of the Temple's Great Hall.

Tibor stood staring down at Will. For a moment, his bushy white eyebrows were knitted together in puzzlement. Then he simply shook his head. Whether or not Tibor agreed with the Oracle, he had to accept his decision.

Will nodded at Tibor and turned around. Her friends instantly rushed toward her, and they all embraced. Will started to feel relief. Then she noticed Yan Lin approaching the group. As the old woman's long white robe brushed the hall's smooth marble floor, Will braced herself for a tongue-lashing.

But when she reached the girls, Yan Lin's serious look was replaced by a smile.

"As they say," she told Will, "you certainly didn't beat around the bush!"

Will wasn't sorry for what she'd done. But she had to admit, she'd taken a major risk. Sheepishly, she shrugged. "I guess I got carried away, didn't I? I just couldn't hold back."

A reassuring hand touched Will's shoulder. Will turned to find Irma looking at her with total admiration. "The Oracle is really unbearable sometimes," she said. "Just a little too often, I'd say!"

Taranee laughed. "We already know how you feel, Irma!"

Just then, the Guardians noticed the sound of chattering all around them. The Elders had formed into little groups. They were speaking to each other softly in hundreds of different languages.

With a worried look, Hay Lin glanced up at the gallery seats. "Are the Elders saying bad things about us?" she asked her grandmother. "They're giving us such strange looks."

Yan Lin's smile broadened. "They're talking about you, but with respect! Nothing like this has ever happened before."

The Guardians all exchanged surprised glances.

"Seeing the Oracle walk off like that, without replying to your criticism, was something new for us," Yan Lin informed them.

A half-dozen Elders with alien features drew closer and nodded their agreement with Yan Lin.

"I say you should stop by more often," a froglike Elder said in a croaking voice. "Sometimes life gets pretty boring around here!"

Will laughed, but nervously. While she was

happy to be the source of entertainment, she preferred that things stay boring in Candracar—at least for a little while. The Guardians had endured enough excitement and upheaval. They needed a break!

THREE

Cornelia watched Tibor descend the steps leading from the Great Hall's golden pedestal. His movements were always full of quiet dignity. "Guardians!" he boomed. "It's your turn now. As soon as Galgheita gets here, you can leave."

Fine, thought Cornelia, I volunteered to do this job, and I'm ready. The sooner I leave, the sooner I can put all this behind me.

She stepped forward, holding her chin high. "I'll take care of it right away," she declared in a strong voice.

Most of her tears had dried by then, but Cornelia swiped angrily at her cheeks anyway, just to make sure. The last thing she wanted was for

Mrs. Rudolph to see that she'd blubbered her eyes out over Caleb.

Just then, Cornelia noticed Yan Lin looking at her. The former Guardian had been watching Cornelia brush her tears away, and her expression suddenly seemed to soften.

"Good luck, Cornelia," Yan Lin said, quickly embracing her.

Cornelia closed her eyes as the old woman hugged her. Yan Lin's spirit was so strong it glowed with a warmth that Cornelia could actually feel. For a moment, the woman's strength of spirit renewed Cornelia's own . . . but only for a moment.

"See you soon, Yan Lin," Cornelia whispered with a weak smile.

The other Guardians hugged Cornelia, too. Then she readied herself for the trip back home.

"See you tomorrow, guys," she said. "I'll send Mrs. Rudolph over and go straight to bed."

Taranee waved. "We'll say hi to Elyon for you, okay?"

"Yeah," Cornelia replied. The thought of Elyon was almost enough to make her change her mind about going. It had been a long time since she'd seen her best friend. She was sorry she had to miss the chance to visit with her again. But she just couldn't bear going, not when Caleb was along for the ride.

"Tell her I miss her like crazy," Cornelia said, resisting the urge to look Caleb's way one last time. Meeting Will's eyes, she nodded. It was time to go.

Will held out her palm and called up the Heart of Candracar. The brilliant amulet shone like a celestial star in Will's hand. As Cornelia shut her eyes and focused her mind on thoughts of earth, the ancient, mystical crystal flashed with a searing light.

When Cornelia opened her eyes again, she was standing under a streetlamp near Heatherfield Park. It took her only a moment to get her bearings. She was right across from the stately granite edifice containing the Heatherfield Museum.

Cornelia glanced around. It was the middle of a cold, dark night, and the streets were deathly quiet. The park's tall trees swayed above the streetlamps, their limbs throwing skeletal shadows on the shrubs and grass. Cornelia shivered, feeling as empty and deserted as the midnight streets.

How could I have been so fooled by Caleb? she asked herself as she strode down a cold, concrete sidewalk. All my dreaming and loving . . . all my caring and waiting . . . all my pining and hoping . . . for what? To be dumped without so much as a second thought?

She shook her head as she walked along, trying to understand what had happened and why. She would have given anything, even her own life, to be with Caleb and keep him safe.

After Nerissa had attacked him and left him for dead, she had taken him to the Oracle. She had begged him to heal the boy she loved. And he had.

He'd placed Caleb in a mysterious room called the Cosmos of Abeyance. For months, Caleb had remained suspended among the healing energies of that strange Temple room. And it had worked. He had regained his memories, his identity, and his strength. He was all right now. He was alive and well. For that, Cornelia knew she *should* be grateful. Even her anger and grief could not wash that away.

Yet she was still sad. She couldn't help thinking of all their happy times together. She replayed the scenes again and again in her head growing sadder and sadder. Without Caleb, Cornelia felt alone, depleted, like a child's party balloon that had lost all its lift. Sure, they had had their challenges—they didn't live in the same town, or even the same world! But she had really believed that they could work through those challenges, together. He was the boy of her dreams. They had fought bravely for Meridian together and had shared many special moments. He had made her feel so happy, and now all she felt was incredibly sad.

"I just can't believe it hurts so much," she murmured. "And what's worse is, it feels like it's never going to stop hurting. . . ."

"Huh?" a voice grunted.

Cornelia halted, her senses suddenly on high alert. Had she just heard a man's voice? She glanced around and saw a pile of newspapers on a park bench. Suddenly the papers shifted, and she realized that a man was lying underneath them.

"Who are you?" asked the man, looking up at her with wide, fearful eyes.

Cornelia blinked, knowing that it would take a long time to explain how she'd suddenly appeared near the park in her Guardian form. The man was gaping at her turquoise wings and glittering outfit, her long blond hair shimmering in the lamplight like the locks of a golden fairy.

"Am I dreaming?" asked the man, sitting up and rubbing his eyes.

Cornelia sighed, not wanting to get involved in a long conversation. "Yes," she finally told him. "You're dreaming."

She was about to turn and walk away, but something inside made her stop to take a closer look at the person sitting in front of her. He wore a ripped red hat and a threadbare coat, and he'd pulled the pile of newspapers over his torso in a vain effort to keep warm on that bone-chilling night.

This man has no home, Cornelia realized. He has no family. She shook her head. Just a moment ago, she'd been pitying herself, telling herself that she was all alone after Caleb had broken up with her. But now that she thought about it, she realized she wasn't really alone. She had friends who cared about her. She had a mother and a father—even a little pest of a sister who would miss her if she never came home again.

And I can go home, thought Cornelia, because, unlike this poor man, I have one.

"Aren't you cold under that?" she asked the man.

"Yeah," he said. "Really cold." Then he smiled at her and shrugged. "But old Ray is used to it."

The man's spirit moved Cornelia. She realized that, on another night, she might have passed him by and not given him a second thought.

But tonight things were different.

Tonight, Cornelia's own heartache had given her something in common with a man like Ray. She suddenly knew, really knew, what it felt like to be kicked around, to be in need and in pain, to feel completely alone in your suffering.

In an instant, she made a decision. After glancing at the park behind her, she briefly closed her eyes. With a deep breath, she connected herself to the elemental currents of the ancient planet, letting its power flow through her bones and muscles.

As the earth Guardian, she was able to feel the pulsing energy of life in the trees and shrubs around her, the grass and earth beneath her feet. When she opened her eyes again, she looked at the homeless man.

"Tell me, Ray," she said softly, "do you believe in magic?"

"In magic?" Ray shook his weary head, showing Cornelia just how many holes were in his knit cap. "Of course not!"

Cornelia smiled. "You really should."

Turning to a small plot of grass, Cornelia extended her arms and focused her power. Bright swirls of green earth magic streamed from her hands as she commanded seeds to germinate instantly, then put down roots and spring from the soil.

As four sturdy tree trunks rose high, Cornelia smiled. Okay, she thought, I've got four good posts for Ray's new house. Now for the walls and roof!

Another burst of green magic commanded vines and shrubs to grow as fast as flashing lightning. They curled around the tree trunk pillars, tangling to form thick walls and a solid roof. Then, leaves grew and flowers blossomed, creating insulation strong enough to block any wind and stop any rain.

When Cornelia withdrew her magic and put down her arms, she stood before the finished structure.

"Who . . . what are you?" asked the homeless man, his eyes wide with shock. "Some kind of fairy?"

Cornelia shrugged. "More or less," she said. Then she stepped back, gesturing for the man to enter the house. Inside, Ray found a lush bed of soft leaves and grass. The smell of flowers was as sweet as perfume.

"Wow," he whispered. His eyes were still wide, but now he was smiling. "Thanks," he told Cornelia. "But why? . . . Why did you do this for me?"

"Because tonight I felt like it," Cornelia said. She wasn't about to tell him about Caleb or her own heartache. But she did say one thing: "This is an act of love."

Then she waved and turned to go. "Sleep well, my friend. Now you have a home, too."

A little while later, Cornelia was standing on the wide wooden porch of Mrs. Rudolph's Victorian house. It was time for her to finish her assignment.

Knock-knock-knock!

The door opened a crack, and a plump, middle-aged woman with big tinted glasses peered through. "Cornelia?"

"Mrs. Rudolph, it's me."

The woman smiled at the blond Guardian and opened the door wide. Cornelia strode in, saying, "They're waiting for you in Candracar, Mrs. Rudolph. Are you ready to go home?"

Mrs. Rudolph clapped her hands. "Oh, my! . . . It's all I've wanted! I just never expected it would happen so soon!"

As part of her cover, Mrs. Rudolph had taught math at Sheffield Institute for several years. She'd been one of the best teachers there, and all the students had loved her. Of course, they'd never guessed her secret. She wasn't human!

Cornelia knew all about the role Mrs. Rudolph had played in Elyon's history. Originally, she'd been a nurse to the young princess Elyon in Metamoor's capital city, Meridian. When Elyon's parents died, her brother, Phobos, took over the kingdom and began a reign of terror. And she had feared that Phobos would try to kill Elyon, as she was the rightful heir.

To keep young Elyon safe from Prince Phobos, Mrs. Rudolph bravely traveled through a portal to Heatherfield with the little girl. Two rebels helped them escape—Alborn and Miriadel. In Heatherfield, they took the names Eleanor and Thomas Brown.

The Browns raised Elyon as their own daughter. And Mrs. Rudolph settled close by, taking a teaching job at Sheffield Institute. Of course, all three of them—Eleanor, Thomas, and Mrs. Rudolph—had changed their appearances to look like human beings. They fit in perfectly in Heatherfield. No one suspected anything strange about them.

Now that Phobos was defeated and Elyon had taken the throne, Mrs. Rudolph could safely return to Meridian. Cornelia could tell that Mrs. Rudolph was elated.

"Where are your suitcases?" Cornelia asked, looking around the woman's tidy bedroom.

"No bags," said Mrs. Rudolph. "Nothing from my terrestrial life could be of use in Meridian. I'm only taking one thing . . . this."

She walked over to her dresser and picked up a framed print of Sheffield Institute.

Cornelia smiled, remembering the day she and Will had purchased that print. All of the students had chipped in to buy Mrs. Rudolph a retirement present. Cornelia and Will had shopped for hours before they found the perfect gift. By the look on Mrs. Rudolph's face, Cornelia could see they'd done a pretty good job. It was the perfect memento.

Mrs. Rudolph gazed at the print for a minute then hugged it to her chest. Seeing a tear slip down the woman's cheek, Cornelia teared up, too.

Farewells were never easy. And that night Cornelia was feeling especially emotional about any and all good-byes.

"Do you want to see it one last time before you leave?" she asked Mrs. Rudolph.

"I'd be delighted to!" The teacher's face lit up for a moment before falling again. "But didn't you say they were waiting for me?"

Cornelia waved a hand. "Oh, they can wait a little while longer."

With the framed print under her arm, Mrs. Rudolph led the way down the stairs and out her front door. She and Cornelia made their way over to the school, which wasn't far away. But they couldn't get in. The front gate was locked.

A minor inconvenience for a Guardian, thought Cornelia. "Follow me," she said.

She led the math teacher to the side of the building, where the iron fence gave way to a stone wall. Closing her eyes, Cornelia concentrated on the energy of the earth. Then she let loose. Extending her arms, she threw out an explosive burst of powerful green magic.

Sh—whammm!

Cornelia gestured toward the huge, perfectly round hole in the thick wall. Mrs. Rudolph could easily step through it and enter the school grounds to look around.

"Go on," she told Mrs. Rudolph. "Take your time."

"I won't be long," the teacher promised. "I just want to say good-bye for the last time."

As Cornelia trailed behind, she noticed something interesting. When Mrs. Rudolph looked up at the building, she appeared sadder than ever. Her eyes were full of tears and her face full of pain.

Then, slowly, her expression began to brighten, and the sadness melted. Mrs. Rudolph seemed to be remembering things that had happened in her past—good things.

"They were such happy years," the teacher murmured. A moment later, she actually laughed!

Cornelia was struck by the transformation. She wondered if she would ever be able to think back on the time she had spent with Caleb and feel good . . . even happy?

It seemed completely ridiculous at the moment. Totally impossible. She couldn't imagine ever feeling good about that boy again. But a part of her held on to the hope that someday it just *might* be possible.

Mrs. Rudolph sighed. "Now I have to go," she murmured, turning to face Cornelia again. "It's time to return to where I came from . . . and to my real appearance."

The teacher closed her eyes, and her form immediately began to change. Her human shape began to grow wider and taller. Her human skin grew scaly and spotted. Her glasses disappeared, and in their place were large, glowing red eyes.

Gradually, she morphed into a large, reptilian alien with a ridged belly. Floppy ears stuck out between the long red locks of hair on her head. Her face turned into a mass of jowls with three red horns protruding from her fleshy neck. Her hands turned into claws, and she grew a long, scaly tail.

Cornelia shivered. The transformation was quite dramatic, and it always took a moment for her to get used to Mrs. Rudolph's real appearance. She took a deep breath and stepped up to her former teacher.

"Good-bye, Mrs. Rudolph," she said, opening her arms for a hug.

The Metamoorian woman smiled and spoke. "There is no Mrs. Rudolph any longer. Now there's only Galgheita."

Cornelia nodded. It was true. Even Mrs. Rudolph's voice was gone. Its tone was now growly and burbly. But Cornelia knew that, inside, the creature standing before her was the same person she knew and loved. She hugged the teacher tight.

"Bye, Galgheita," she said. Then Cornelia stepped back. "In a moment, you'll be far away," she warned. "Close your eyes . . . and open them only when you get to Candracar."

Galgheita did as Cornelia said. Then the blond Guardian extended her arms, concentrating on her powers.

Once more, Cornelia's bright green earth magic flowed through her body and out her fingertips with magnified power. The crackling force surrounded Galgheita, and in a single, blinding flash, she was gone.

FOUR

Taranee folded her arms and tapped her foot. For the past hour, she'd been watching Caleb pace back and forth across the Great Hall's mist-shrouded floor.

He obviously can't wait to get back to his home, she thought.

And while she wanted to, she couldn't begrudge him that. He and Mrs. Rudolph had been away from Meridian for a long time. Taranee couldn't imagine being away from her parents and her brother for that long. In a way, she felt sorry for Caleb—yet not *too* sorry. After all, she had seen the pained look on Cornelia's face before she'd left Candracar.

Speaking of which, what was taking Cornelia so long? Taranee wondered.

Not that she blamed her. How could she not want to get as far away from Caleb as possible after he had broken her heart? If Nigel ever pulled that on her, she didn't know what she'd do. Thinking about her own love, Taranee sighed heavily.

It hadn't always been easy with Nigel. Sure, they were in the same school and they were both from Heatherfield, but they were from very different groups of friends. Still, Taranee couldn't help liking the sweet boy. She knew that he was just mixed up with the wrong people. Uriah, Kurt, and Laurent were bad news. When Nigel got into trouble along with the other boys, Taranee's mother, Judge Cook, had gotten involved. After that happened, her mother was adamant that Taranee should stay away from Nigel. It took a long time to get her mother to see how different Nigel was from the other boys . . . and that he deserved a second chance to prove he was really a good guy. Now things were great with Nigel and her mother. Taranee smiled. She knew how lucky she was to have him.

With a little sigh, the fire Guardian closed her eyes and sent Cornelia a private, telepathic message: "Take all the time you need. We've got your back. We always will."

Taranee shook her head. It was really sad that Cornelia was going to miss seeing her best friend, Elyon. She and Elyon had been really tight back in Heatherfield, *before* Elyon had found out the truth about her own identity.

How strange it must have been for Elyon to learn that her whole Heatherfield life had been a sham, that she was really a queen in another world. Her mother and father weren't really her mom and dad. And her math teacher was in on the whole thing!

It hadn't stopped there.

Once Elyon returned to Metamoor, her own older brother and his snakelike servant, Cedric, had manipulated her in all sorts of ways. They'd lied to her. They'd made her trust them while they actually plotted to destroy her and steal her magic. For a while, they even made her believe that the Guardians were evil—that her old friends were, in fact, her worst enemies.

Taranee shuddered at one particular memory of Metamoor, when she'd been captured and imprisoned in Prince Phobos's castle. The evil bounty hunter, Frost, had caught her while she and the other Guardians were trying to escape. What a total nightmare that had been!

Like some lab specimen, Taranee had been sealed in a clear bubble and left to float at the bottom of a dark stone turret. And that wasn't even the worst of it! Elyon had visited Taranee. She had whispered cruel things, trying to convince her that Will and the others had abandoned her.

Elyon had shown Taranee a vision of the astral drop the Guardians had created—a twin that looked and acted just like Taranee. Elyon claimed that the Guardians were going to let Astral Taranee take the real Taranee's place . . . forever.

Thank goodness I never stopped believing in the power of friendship! Taranee thought.

Of course, Will and the others did finally come to her rescue. And Taranee's power over fire helped her melt her own bubble prison and break free.

Forgiving Elyon for her behavior back then had been hard. But Taranee knew the girl had been misled, lied to, and exploited.

It's sort of like how the Oracle treats us sometimes, Taranee joked to herself. But only to herself. The Oracle was one powerful dude, and he'd already had an earful tonight, thanks to Will!

Anyway, the only thing that Taranee truly regretted about her time on Metamoor was not being able to give Phobos a flaming taste of his own medicine. In her view, that dude deserved to kiss a fireball for all he'd done. But Taranee never got the chance to overheat him. Elyon's own powers did that. Little sister had really kicked her big bro's behind!

In the end, however, Elyon chose not to destroy him. Instead, she subdued him, binding him with magical ropes and leaving him for the Oracle to deal with. The wise seer wasted no time in punishing Phobos and his sidekick, Cedric. Both of them were transported to Candracar and locked in the Tower of Mists. It was a prison from which no one could leave—unless the Oracle said so.

Taranee began to pace the floor of the Great Hall. It's funny, she told herself, how returning to a particular place can stir up all sorts of memories, both good and bad. Phobos and his evil henchmen certainly didn't leave me many good ones. But now that they're gone, Meridian may not be so bad.

And seeing Elyon again was sure to bring up some good memories. Taranee often wondered how the girl had been doing since they had defeated Phobos. Being a queen had to be a lot cooler than going to classes at Sheffield!

Just then, a blinding light appeared in front of Taranee. She shaded her eyes and looked closer. In the center of the brilliance was the silhouette of a large figure. As the light faded, Taranee made out a ridged tummy, a long tail, a jowly face, floppy ears, and red dreadlocks. In the creature's arms was a framed picture of Sheffield Institute.

"Oh . . . here already!" cried the creature, hugging the frame to her wide, ridged torso.

It's Mrs. Rudolph, Taranee realized. She's arrived in Candracar! Except, I guess she's not Mrs. Rudolph anymore. She's back to her regular form as Galgheita.

Will stepped forward to greet the retired math teacher. "Did you have a good trip, ma'am?" she asked.

"Oh, my, yes," Galgheita replied. "How wonderful this is! I can't wait to go home again!"

Taranee smiled, hearing the excited tone in Galgheita's voice.

Irma walked over to Taranee. "I guess Cornelia didn't change her mind," she said in a low voice. "She said she'd be staying in Heatherfield, and she stuck to her word."

Taranee waved her hand. "You should know the earth girl by now, Irma. Our friend is one tough cookie!"

Just then, Tibor approached Will and Galgheita. He called Caleb and the rest of the Guardians closer. "The passage leading to Meridian is ready to welcome you," he said. "Farewell, Guardians."

Will smiled. "See you soon, Tibor."

"Yeah, and when you need a hand," Irma joked, "just whistle." She stuck two fingers in her mouth to demonstrate. Then she pulled them out and added, "But not too soon, please!"

Taranee laughed. Yeah, she thought, I've got to agree with Irma on that one. W.I.T.C.H. has definitely earned some time off!

Tibor shook his head. The water Guardian

never ceased to amaze him. "I long for the time when I'm finally accustomed to your informal ways," he said.

Tibor's voice sounded totally weary, but Taranee could see the amusement in the old man's eyes.

A moment later, Yan Lin moved forward to say farewell. Smiling warmly, she put one arm around Will and the other around Irma.

"I know I've already told you this," said the old woman, "but I'm proud of you all. Of who you are and everything you've done."

Taranee felt her eyes fill with tears and knew that the other girls were also struggling not to cry. Since no one knew what they did, it was rare for them to get compliments. And the fact that the praise came from Yan Lin made it all the more special. Finally, Hay Lin composed herself and said, "Thanks, Grandma."

"Farewell for now, girls," said Yan Lin. After one last hug of her granddaughter, she stepped back.

Will glanced at Tibor, and he nodded. A moment later, Taranee saw a pinpoint of light appear at their feet. The tiny glow grew larger until its brightness encompassed the entire group—the four Guardians, Caleb, and Galgheita.

Then, in one dazzling flash, the beam of light embraced them. Taranee's eyes squinted as its brilliance surrounded her. Her entire body tingled—every muscle, every molecule. Her feet were no longer touching the ground, and she felt completely weightless. But she wasn't floating. She was moving at great speed, like a crackling pulse in an electric current. And the current wasn't flowing through her or around her. She felt as if *she* were the current, as if she'd become part of the beam itself!

This journey was awesome. It was nothing like her rough-and-tumble travels through the portals. Taranee remembered how she'd been thrown around during those journeys from Heatherfield to Meridian. There'd been a good reason for that. The portals had actually been formed by accidents. They were unauthorized gateways created by random rips in the Veil, so there had been nothing smooth about those passages.

The light she traveled on now was part of an ancient transport system. The people of

Candracar had used it from the time the universe had first taken shape. Even now, Taranee was racing by some of the worlds the Oracle watched over.

Because of the speed at which they were traveling, most of those worlds were nothing but blurs. Yet in the space of a few seconds, Taranee glimpsed the most amazing sights.

There was a sand world, covered with anthill cities, whose citizens resembled bugs. There was a world of levitating farms with crops planted in the clouds. There was even a dimension of giant, birdlike beings that lived in tree houses!

In a few short moments, however, it was all over. The magical beam of light had swept them from the Temple, in the center of infinity, over an interdimensional bridge, and into one of the thousands of worlds protected by Candracar.

Taranee felt her feet touch the ground again. She blinked and took a deep breath. Her limbs were still tingling from the journey, and her eyes still felt blinded by the dazzling light. Within moments, the bright, tingling glow faded away, and she could make out the sights around her.

She saw tall, Gothic buildings of old stone. There were humanlike people, but also green and blue creatures who clearly weren't human. They were of all shapes and sizes, with pointy ears and gremlin faces, and they wore cloaks and boots or headscarves and peasant dresses.

Farmers and city dwellers alike were gawking at the Guardians. Taranee wasn't surprised. It wasn't every day that one saw four winged girls and a rebel hero materialize in a flash, right before one's eyes.

But that's exactly what has happened, Taranee thought. We're back in Meridian!

FIVE

In her majestic home of stone and stained glass, Elyon sat at the large oak table in the palace library. Thousands of books crammed the shelves around her.

There were books about Metamoor's history and about its art and architecture. There were books about the flora and fauna of Metamoor. And there were stories, thousands of them, based on Metamoor's colorful legends and folk-tales.

As the brand-new queen of Meridian, Elyon was expected to read every one of those books. But first she had to learn the Metamoorian language. And reading any language started with one very basic lesson—learning its alphabet.

"Let's try that again, Your Highness," said the tutor standing beside her. "But this time I won't show the letters to you in order."

Elyon's private teacher wore a long blue gown and a tall hat that coiled at one end in a curlicue. Her ears were pointy, and her skin was the color of an avocado. None of these strange features bothered Elyon. What bothered the young queen was the simple fact that her teacher never smiled!

"What letter is this?" asked the teacher. She pointed to the open book in front of Elyon.

Elyon flipped back one of her straw-blond braids and flashed a teasing grin. "Could I have a hint?" she asked.

The teacher frowned. "I beg your pardon."

"A hint," Elyon repeated with a shrug. "On TV game shows they always give hints. It's a sort of . . . helping hand."

"I don't understand," said the teacher.

Elyon blinked her large blue eyes. "I imagine you've never seen a game show, have you?"

"You imagine correctly, Your Majesty," the teacher said with a proud sniff.

Elyon tried not to laugh. She'd been born in Metamoor, but she'd grown up in Heatherfield—

with TV, fast food, and the Sheffield Institute. There was a lot she still had to learn about this place. That was one reason the royal court had assigned her a tutor.

Always a pretty good student, Elyon wasn't too worried about learning everything she needed to know. She'd gotten good grades at Sheffield. And when she applied herself, she picked things up pretty fast.

Plus, she thought, I've already learned the most important lesson about being a new queen. I've learned to love the world I govern.

That had proved easy for Elyon. She loved the people of Metamoor, and she loved the beautiful countryside, bustling towns, and fruitful farms. Her powers had grown even stronger with that love. She happily stretched her magical energies over the land to protect and nourish her people.

Never again would she allow Metamoor to suffer under the rule of someone evil, like her brother. Never again would she allow her world to darken the way it had during Phobos's reign.

"Elyon?" called a gentle voice.

The queen looked up to find a familiar female standing in the library doorway. She had pale green skin, wide eyes, and long blue dreadlocks. She wore a white gown and, on her face, an expression of urgency.

"Pardon the intrusion, Your Highness," said the female, bowing her head. "I didn't realize you were busy."

"What is it, Mom?" Elyon asked with a smile. Then she caught herself. "I . . . um . . . mean, Captain Miriadel?"

Elyon still slipped sometimes and called Miriadel "Mom." She did the same with Alborn, the commander of the Royal Guard of Meridian. Sometimes she still called him "Dad."

Of course, everyone understood why Elyon did that. Miriadel and Alborn had been her adoptive parents in Heatherfield and in charge of her well-being during her time of refuge there. For most of her life, they were the only family she knew. It made sense that she still occasionally slipped.

Elyon was fully aware of the sacrifices that Miriadel, Alborn, and her nurse, Galgheita, had made for her, the way they risked their lives to protect her. It must not have been easy to execute a plan to kidnap a baby princess! But they were brave and loyal, and they had managed to pull it off. To fit in in Heatherfield, they'd changed not only their names, but their appearances as well. Certainly that hadn't been an easy feat for them, either.

It must have been weird for them to morph into humans, Elyon thought. For as strange as pale green skin and blue dreadlocks seemed to her, brown hair and human skin tones were probably very strange to them. However, they never complained, but simply did their best to adapt to the community. Elyon knew she would always be incredibly grateful for all of their love and support.

Miriadel stepped closer, and Elyon snapped back to the present. "There's something going on in the city that you should see."

"Really?" Elyon's blue eyes widened in curiosity.

Even the stern teacher appeared curious. "We'll continue our lesson after a short break, then," she announced with great formality.

Miriadel cleared her throat. "Um . . . I've got the impression it won't be so short!"

Now Elyon was *really* curious! What could it be? she wondered. She quickly rose from her royal chair, carved in wood and upholstered in royal purple. Smoothing her lilac silk-and-satin gown, she nodded to Miriadel.

"Lead the way," she declared.

Miriadel smiled. "I've already called for the coach, Your Highness."

Within minutes, Elyon's royal coach pulled up to the palace entrance. The footmen helped Elyon and Miriadel into the plush interior. When they both were settled in their seats, the driver shook the reins, and the six strong red steeds galloped off.

They raced through the palace gates. Elyon was getting nervous. What was all this mystery? Following the descending road, they flew down to the bustling center of Meridian. There Elyon saw that the people of Meridian were laughing and shouting; the children were jumping and dancing.

"Wow, what's going on here?" Elyon murmured.

Obviously, some sort of celebration was taking place. Was this one of the Metamoorian holidays that she had failed to memorize?

The driver had already slowed the royal coach considerably. Now the horses were trotting gently through the packed streets. A mob had gathered in a circle at the center of the outdoor market. The driver directed Elyon's coach toward the center of the commotion.

Suddenly someone shouted, "Elyon!"

The queen thought she recognized the voice. It sounded just like Will Vandom!

Elyon popped open the coach door. That was when she saw that all of her old friends were there! Hay Lin, Taranee, and Irma were standing near Will.

"Guys!" she cried, rushing over and giving them each a big hug. Elyon didn't see Cornelia, but she assumed her best friend was there, too—just lost somewhere in the crazy crowd.

"This sure is a surprise," Elyon told them. She gestured around her. "But what's going on here? Who's having a party?"

Will laughed. "We just gave a ride to a couple of people," she explained.

Hay Lin grinned. "And it looks like they're pretty popular around these parts."

"Who do you mean?" Elyon asked.

Hay Lin jerked her thumb in the direction of the hooting crowd. Elyon looked closer and finally saw them. Two beloved Metamoorians were being hugged and kissed by dozens of fellow citizens.

"Caleb! Mrs. Rud—er, I mean, Galgheita!" Elyon exclaimed.

When Galgheita heard her queen's voice, she broke from the crowd and stepped forward. "Your Highness," she said, bowing her head respectfully.

Caleb also approached. He put a hand to his heart. "Light of Meridian," he said, bowing deeply.

My teacher and my courageous rebel champion, Elyon thought. I'm so thrilled to see them both!

With her two delicate hands, she gripped Caleb's strong ones and squeezed them tight.

"Caleb," she said in amazement, "I'm so happy you're safe! Phobos turned you into a flower. How did you manage to break his spell?"

Caleb's liquid brown eyes clouded for a moment. "It's a long story, Elyon."

She smiled. "Oh, I'm in no hurry. There are so many things you have to tell me about!"

In her mind, Elyon was already planning a grand welcoming banquet and ball. Caleb had risked his life to help her regain her throne, and she had every intention of showing him her appreciation.

Elyon turned to Galgheita. She grinned at her former math teacher, trying to imagine what the kids at Sheffield would have said if they could have seen her now, with her strange, floppy ears; red dreadlocks; big, ridged tummy; and thick, long tail!

"I'm so glad to see both of you!" Elyon cried, drawing them into her arms. "It's wonderful to have you back." Elyon gave Caleb and Galgheita a big, warm hug. Then she began to glance around. She counted up the Guardians again—Will, Irma, Taranee, Hay Lin . . . but still, no Cornelia.

Why is my best friend missing? she wondered. She turned to Will. "So, where's Cornelia?"

For a moment, Will's face fell. "Cornelia had to—uh—go back to Heatherfield," she said, "but, uh, she says hi!"

Elyon couldn't believe her ears. Cornelia had *promised* to come back to Meridian for a visit. It didn't make any sense for the other Guardians to be there and not her. And from the look on Will's face, it was clear she was upset about it, too.

"Did something happen back home?" Elyon asked. "Is her family okay?"

"Yes, Elyon. They're all fine. But—uh—nothing happened. . . ." Will seemed to be forcing a big smile as she glanced at the other Guardians. "Right?"

"Right!" said Irma, stepping up. A big smile now appeared on her face, too. "Nothing happened. Nothing at all."

Elyon glanced at Hay Lin and Taranee. The two were vigorously nodding their heads in agreement.

"My dear Elyon," Galgheita interrupted, "how are you getting on as the new queen?"

Elyon turned toward her old teacher. "Very well!" she assured her. "I'm so happy here . . . except for one thing."

"Oh? What's that?" Galgheita asked.

"I've missed you," said Elyon, giving her another big hug. "I never imagined I'd be so happy to see my math teacher again. It's okay if I call you Galgheita, right?"

Galgheita laughed. "You have to! It's an order, if I'm allowed to say that."

Elyon nodded. "You know, now that I'm grown-up, I don't need a nurse anymore. But I'd be honored to have you at the castle as my personal tutor."

"Your tutor?" Galgheita looked pleased.

Elyon's expression turned grave. "Only *you* can save me from the heartless teacher they found for me!"

Miriadel leaned toward Elyon. "I think there's room for *both*," she declared.

With a sigh, Elyon realized she'd just assigned herself *two* private teachers. And they were probably going to make her study twice as much.

"Now you've done it," Taranee told Elyon with a laugh. "There's no turning back."

Just then, another shout went up. "Look! It's Caleb!" cried one member of a group of big blue men. They were farmers who'd just arrived from out of town.

"It's true, Caleb's returned!" exclaimed someone from yet another newly arrived group.

"*Caleb! Caleb! Caleb!*" chanted the crowd.

Caleb turned to his queen. "May I go to them, Your Highness?"

The queen grinned and nodded. If anyone

deserved a glorious homecoming, it was this brave warrior. "They're all yours, Caleb," she told him.

As the handsome young hero moved into the chanting crowd, Elyon's heart filled with joy.

I don't know where Cornelia is or why she didn't come to visit, she thought. But I'm so very happy that Caleb and Galgheita have returned to their true home.

SIX

Hay Lin shook her head as she watched Caleb move toward his chanting fans.

It's a good thing Cornelia didn't come with us after all, she decided. Seeing Caleb treated as a returning hero after what he did to her would have been way harsh . . . and really hard for Cornelia to handle.

"Caleb!" cried a giant blue man.

"Vathek, old friend!" Caleb shouted.

Hay Lin smiled as she saw Vathek's familiar grin. He had been a major ally in the fight against Phobos. He was obviously thrilled to be having this reunion with Caleb. The two came together like colliding freight trains, and Caleb was quickly swallowed up by Vathek's big, blue hug.

"Hey, you big brute," called a blue female creature behind Vathek. "Leave a bit of him for us."

"Nothing doing," said Vathek, patting Caleb's shaggy brown head. "It's my turn now!"

When Vathek finally released the rebel leader, the crowd lifted him up and cheered. Then they began to chant again. *"Caleb! Caleb! Caleb!"*

Elyon laughed and leaned toward the Guardians. "What ingrates," she joked. "Up until today, I was their favorite."

Will smiled at that.

But Irma didn't, and Elyon took notice.

Hay Lin watched as Elyon's face grew worried. It was clear the queen had expected to hear one of Irma's trademark sarcastic responses.

"What's the matter, Irma?" Elyon asked. "Do you think I should start worrying about his popularity?"

Irma narrowed her eyes as she looked at the young rebel leader. The crowd was happily parading him around on their shoulders. "If I were you," Irma said, "I'd lock him up in prison for a century or two."

Hay Lin folded her arms and nodded.

"That's not a bad idea. People change very quickly."

Elyon stared at for them a second, then waved her hand and laughed. "Shame on you! You shouldn't even joke about such things!"

Elyon turned back to Will, and Irma exchanged a glance with Hay Lin. "Who was kidding?" Irma whispered.

"I sure wasn't!" Hay Lin said. After what Caleb had done to Cornelia, the last thing she would have given him was a celebration like this.

Trying to imagine how she'd have felt if Eric had ever broken her heart the way Caleb had broken Cornelia's, Hay Lin found that she couldn't even begin to go to such a dark place. It made her sad to even *think* of such a terrible thing. To have actually gone through it would have been torture.

I'd never be able to forgive Eric, she determined. I'd probably unleash a hurricane on him—or at least a tornado!

Clearly, Cornelia has a more mature outlook than I do, Hay Lin decided. Cornelia didn't even use her magic on Caleb, which is too bad. I can just see Caleb now, trapped inside the hollow trunk of a five-hundred-year-old oak!

That notion alone made the air Guardian's frown turn upside down.

"Caleb! Caleb! Caleb!" the crowd continued to chant.

Elyon turned to Will. "I hope you'll be sticking around for a while this time," she said.

Will shook her head. "We're really sorry, Elyon, but we have to run this time, too."

"Oh," said Elyon, clearly disappointed. "That's too bad."

"But we'll come back soon. I promise," Will said, giving Elyon a warm hug. "And next time, Cornelia will be with us."

Will quickly stepped away from Elyon and motioned for the other Guardians to follow her.

"Wait," said Elyon. "You're leaving, just like that?" She gestured toward the celebrating crowd. "Aren't you going to say good-bye to Caleb?"

"No," Will said flatly. "We'll just, uh . . . let him enjoy the celebration in his honor."

"Yeah," Hay Lin told Elyon. "Say good-bye to him for us. We're *sure* he'll understand."

Before Elyon could ask any more questions, the Guardians gathered close together on a patch of Meridian sidewalk. Holding hands, they closed their eyes, and Will called on the power of the Heart—

SHA-WAAAAM!

Hay Lin blinked. In a few short seconds, the Heart's radiant, magical light had burst and faded. The Guardians were still standing on a sidewalk, but they weren't in Metamoor any longer. They were back in Heatherfield.

The old stone buildings of Meridian had been replaced by the modern, glassy skyscrapers of their hometown, and the boisterous crowds were completely gone. The raucous midday celebration had turned into a quiet city night.

The girls weren't in their Guardian forms anymore, either. Their wings were gone, and their bodies were once again younger, smaller, and weaker. Their dazzling purple-and-turquoise outfits were gone, too. Now, they were bundled in the same jeans, sweaters, and coats they'd been wearing when they took off a few days earlier, to defend Candracar from the evil sorceress Nerissa.

Taking a deep breath, Hay Lin smiled. She felt . incredibly relieved to be back in Heatherfield again. And, clearly, Irma felt the same way, because Hay Lin heard her release a very loud sigh.

"It's really over, isn't it?" Irma asked.

Will nodded. "It's so hard to believe. I'm totally exhausted. I can't wait to go back home and put my head on my pillow!"

The girls started to walk down the sidewalk.

Irma shook her head. "I hate to wake my astral drop in the middle of the night," she said, referring to the doubles of themselves that they had made so that no one would notice they were gone.

"I'm not sorry in the least," Taranee muttered.

Hay Lin had to agree. Astral drops carried memories and emotions. They were thinking beings, too. But as far as she was concerned, her astral drop wasn't a real person.

Not even close, she thought. Astral Hay Lin is just a stand-in for the real me when I'm busy doing important save-the-world things.

"I'm tempted to send mine off to school in my place tomorrow!" Hay Lin told the others.

Behind her glasses, Taranee narrowed her brown eyes. "Do it at your own risk," she warned, shaking her finger at Hay Lin. "They probably wouldn't be happy about that in Candracar!"

"Let's take advantage of the time we have left to sleep, then," said Will, heading off from the group. "Good night, guys!"

"Sweet dreams, Will!" Irma called.

"You bet!" Will replied, giving one last wave. "Now that Nerissa's gone, my dreams will certainly be sweet . . . and relaxing!"

Hay Lin laughed. Will sure was right about that one. Nerissa had been a total nightmare— in more ways than one. She would appear to the girls in their dreams and make their slumber a restless and scary event—especially for Will. Now that the wicked woman was gone, things were bound to go smoother for W.I.T.C.H., in dreams and reality.

"Good night, Will!" Hay Lin called.

At least we know that we can all have a peaceful night's rest, she thought.

The Guardians deserved that—and Hay Lin, for one, was ready to hit her bed and to drift off to sleep without fear.

SEVEN

Will smiled as she walked down her street. Everything looked so different in the early morning hours. Almost all the lights were off in the apartment buildings around her. And there wasn't one car rolling by.

It's so strange to see the city deserted like this, she thought. I've never heard such silence in Heatherfield before.

There were no pedestrians, no dogs barking or children shouting and playing. There was just the sound of her footsteps on the cold concrete and the breath of a chilly breeze, tousling her mop of bright red hair.

Shivering, Will shoved her bare hands deeper into her coat pockets. It's colder at this hour, too, she thought, shivering ever so slightly.

The long stretches between streetlights were a little unnerving. The trees and shrubs cast creepy shadows. Will knew deep down that her imagination made things seem scarier at night, but still, she quickened her steps as she walked toward the building up ahead.

"Luckily, I'm almost home—" she whispered, and then she stopped dead.

The entire side of her apartment building was dark, except for one set of windows. "Oh, no," Will murmured. "The lights are still on in my apartment!"

Will hurried toward the building. Once again, she stopped and stared. Parked by the curb was a police car with its emergency lights flashing.

"What's going on?" Will murmured.

Her stomach flip-flopped, and she took off, sprinting toward the front steps of the building. She had a terrible feeling.

"Hey! Young lady!" called a man's voice from behind her.

Will glanced over her shoulder. A heavyset police officer with a thick mustache was right on her heels, but Will refused to stop.

No . . . no . . . no, she thought, bursting into her building. I've got to make sure everything's okay at home!

She ignored the elevator and took the stairs two at a time. All the way up to her floor, she kept thinking about her mother. What good was saving the universe if you couldn't keep your own mom from harm?

When she reached her apartment door, she saw that it was unlocked and stood open a crack.

Will's stomach turned over again, this time with dread. If . . . if . . . anything's happened to her, she thought, I'll never forgive myself. Never!

Will pushed the door all the way open and slowly stepped into the foyer. A police officer stood there. He turned and gaped at Will for a moment.

"Hey!" he called into the living room. "Look who's here!"

Will ignored the man and walked past him into the living room.

Will's mother was sitting on the couch. She glanced up and locked eyes with her daughter for a long moment. Then she seemed to recover.

"Will!" she shouted at the top of her lungs.

Will hesitantly stepped a little closer. Her mom looked a mess. Her long, dark hair was tangled; her brown eyes were filled with tears. She seemed pale and shaky. In a chair across from her, an older policeman held a small notebook and a pen. It looked as though he had been taking copious notes.

Suddenly Will heard someone huffing and puffing behind her. She glanced over her shoulder and saw the heavyset officer from the street who'd called out to her. He was in no shape to race up stairs, but he obviously had. Sweeping a hand over his sweaty forehead, he followed Will right into the living room and now looked down at her with a grim expression on his face.

"Will, where have you been?" her mother demanded.

Where have I been? Will repeated to herself. That was when it hit her. Her astral drop must have gone missing!

"Do you realize it's two in the morning?" her mother snapped. She gestured to the police. "I'm sure you can guess how worried I've been! What you put me through!"

Will was speechless. The whole point of the

astral drop was to prevent *exactly* this sort of thing from happening. Will had conjured her up before going off to join the rest of the group to fight Nerissa. The drop was supposed to stick around Heatherfield . . . and behave!

For a second, Will didn't know what to say to her mother. And that was *not* a good thing— because her mother looked as though she were not in any mood to wait around for an answer.

Just then, the older officer stepped up to Will's mom and placed a hand on her shoulder. "What's important is that she's back home, safe and sound, Mrs. Vandom," he said in a soft, soothing voice.

Whether it was the policeman's words or the steadiness of his hand on her shoulder, her mom seemed to calm down.

As her mother visibly relaxed, Will's heart began to race. Where was her astral drop? If she wasn't there, she could be anywhere in Heatherfield, causing trouble. Her astral drop had gotten her into bad situations before, but this was worse than she could have ever imagined. Will had to find her. She had a sudden panic attack as she recalled her last episode with her double. The silly astral drop had kissed her crush, Matt Olsen! Now, that had been superembarrassing and it had taken a bit of maneuvering to recover from the awkward situation. Luckily, Matt had been very cool about the whole thing. But that didn't mean someone else would be as cool.

"Sergeant Carlton," her mother said, glancing at the younger cop, "I'm sorry to have caused you so much trouble."

"No trouble at all!" said the younger cop. "We were just doing our jobs."

The sergeant nodded. "That's right. That's what we're here for."

As her mother walked all three officers to the front door, Will stayed behind in the living room. She could hear them talking as they moved into the foyer.

"If I can give you some advice," the sergeant said to her mom, "don't be too hard on your daughter."

Her mom gave a loud sigh. "Well, I can't give you my word on that. In any case, thank you for everything."

"Good night," said the policemen.

Will got up and went to the hall. She

watched her mother shut the front door and lean against it. Mrs. Vandom pressed her cheek against the wood and closed her eyes, as if she were about to pass out right there.

Sheepishly Will approached her. "Mom?" she called softly, puzzled at her mother's sudden stillness. "I can explain."

"Explain?" Mrs. Vandom said, her eyes still closed, her face still pressed against the door. "What is there to explain?"

"Well . . . I . . . I don't know, I guess . . ." Will stammered.

With a deep breath her mother opened her eyes and faced her daughter. Suddenly, Will understood why her mother had been leaning against the door. She'd been gathering her energy for the coming war!

Will's mother's brown eyes flashed with outrage. Her hands closed in fists, and her whole body went rigid. "When I came in to wish you good night, your room was empty," she said. "You said you'd be staying in and reading all night long, and instead you sneaked out like a thief! *Where were you?*"

Will sighed and looked down at her scuffed sneakers. What am I going to tell her? she asked herself. The truth would be difficult to explain, and impossible to believe.

"I asked you a question, Will!" her mother shouted, in a tone so harsh Will took a step back.

Will didn't want to lie to her mother, but it seemed she had little choice. Her mother was totally freaking.

"There was a Cobalt Blue concert," Will said. She swallowed uneasily, hating what she was doing. "It was at a club downtown, and . . . and . . . so . . ."

Throwing up her hands, her mother let loose on her. "So you thought it'd be a great idea to go without telling me, without asking for my permission, which you probably would have gotten if you had only asked!"

Will shook her head. "I did it without thinking, Mom." Her voice was pleading, desperate for forgiveness. But her mother wasn't in the mood to forgive. She'd obviously just had the scare of her life. And she was furious with Will for putting her through it.

"I'm disappointed, Will," she said. "I thought I could trust you. True, there used to be problems between us, but I thought we'd cleared them all up by now." She put her hands on her hips and glared. "It looks like I was wrong about that."

Will was devastated. She and her mother had endured a rocky relationship for a very long time, ever since they had moved to Heatherfield. Things had gotten a little weird when her mom had started dating Will's history teacher. Mr. Collins was a nice guy, but—boyfriend material for her mother? That was just bizarre! And then there was the time her mother was going to transfer to another office in a town far from Heatherfield. Though her mother thought she was helping Will out by moving away, she was making Will's life worse. No way could Will leave Heatherfield and her fellow Guardians!

But lately the climate had improved in the Vandom home. Things had really gotten better between them. They hadn't been fighting as much, and they'd both been trying harder to do nice things for each other and get along—until now.

That astral drop! Will thought. She's ruined everything . . . everything!

Will threw up her hands, then grasped the

sides of her head, squeezing handfuls of her hair in frustration. She was exhausted and near tears, and all she wanted to do was tell her mother the truth. *It's not my fault!* she wanted to shout. *But I can't tell you about it!*

"Aaagh!" Will cried.

Of course, Will's mother couldn't hear her daughter's thoughts. All she could see was Will grabbing her own head. All she could hear was Will's desperate wail.

"Please spare me the dramatics, Will," she warned. "Go to bed! It's late, and you've got school tomorrow."

Realizing it would do no good to argue, Will dragged herself to her bedroom. She opened the door, and for a second, she was actually surprised. It all looked the same: the bed; the desk; the pictures and posters; and her favorite froggy slippers, the bedcovers, and the stuffed animals.

"Thank goodness," she whispered.

She hadn't been away for more than a few days, measured in Heatherfield time. But after everything she'd been through in Candracar, it felt more as if she'd been gone for weeks. And it was really hard to believe everything was right there where she'd left it. But it sure was a welcome sight!

Will turned to find her mom standing in the doorway, strangling the doorknob with her hand. She was obviously still very upset. "I'm really sorry," Will said, trying once more to break through her mother's anger.

For a moment, her mother seemed to actually hear her daughter. She blinked, her eyes welling up with tears as she met Will's gaze. But then she looked away, and her angry voice came back.

"I hope you had fun tonight, because your little prank is going to cost you dearly," she promised. "You're grounded, and you can't use your cell phone, either."

Her mother marched over to Will's shelf and snatched the phone. She removed the back and reached inside.

"I'll keep the SIM card for the time being," she said. "Since you'll be spending a lot of time in the house, you'll only be using the home phone."

SLAM!

The door closed. Will's mother was gone, and all the anger and noise had gone with her.

She slammed around in the other room for a few minutes, and then finally the apartment fell as silent as the midnight streets of Heatherfield.

Will just stood there, in the middle of her bedroom, feeling too numb to think, too tired to cry.

If only my best friends could see me now, she thought ruefully. They'd probably wonder why they ever let me be in charge of anything. I am completely spent and one hundred per-cent empty.

Slowly, she sank onto the bed. The fluffy pillow against the headboard began to move. A furry little creature with a bushy tail, cute whiskers, and big, curious eyes emerged from behind it.

The dormouse scampered over to Will, and she scratched its little round ears. "I'm trapped, dormouse," she whispered to her pet. "This is a hopeless situation." In despair, she dropped her head into her hands. "What happened to my astral drop? She was supposed to stay here until I got back!"

Why had she run away? Will silently asked herself. And, more important, *where* had she gone? She must have left when Will's mom was still at home and not made any noise.

"She might have simply disappeared," Will whispered, lifting her head with hope. "I created her when my powers were still weak. Maybe the astral drop just dissolved earlier than planned. . . . But if that's what happened, it means the others had the same problem. I'll just ask them about it the next time I see them."

Will arose from the bed and walked to the window. The nighttime streets didn't look quite so scary from the safety of her bedroom. She looked down at Heatherfield, trying to imagine her double walking around out there some-where—along with Irma's, Cornelia's, Hay Lin's, and Taranee's!

"What a mess!" exclaimed Will.

She considered tiptoeing out into the living room to use the phone. She could call all the Guardians and find out whether their astral drops had gone missing, too. But she quickly gave up on that idea.

It's too late to make a round of phone calls now, she decided. Tomorrow at school I'll find out more.

As she gazed out the window, Will noticed how much darker the street appeared. Thick clouds had moved in over the city. In the distance, a crackling bolt of lightning lit up the night sky.

A storm was coming, Will realized. And an unhappy chill went straight through her.

EIGHT

The chilly night gave way to a bright, warm morning. Cornelia opened her eyes, feeling good. And then she remembered. . . .

Caleb broke up with me.

"Nothing like an uplifting thought to get you out of bed in the morning," she muttered.

For a second, Cornelia actually considered *staying* in bed. Hiding under the covers sounded pretty good just then. She considered rolling over and pretending that her alarm hadn't gone off. But she was honest with herself, and knew that that wouldn't make the pain go away. And neither would brooding about it all day long.

My best friends, Cornelia thought, that's what I need. And school—to get my mind on something other than Caleb.

Throwing off her covers, she padded to the bathroom. As usual, she brushed her teeth, took a shower, did her hair. Every action was the same as it ever was, except for one thing. Before this, whenever she brushed her teeth, took a shower, and did her hair, she had always thought about her relationship with Caleb.

How many times a day did I daydream about him? she wondered. Dozens? Hundreds?

She would replay their moments together. Or she'd invent amazing new ones for them to share in the future.

Now the dreams were over. They were all gone. And she felt totally empty, numb, and hollow, with no way to replace them. Just then, she caught a glimpse of herself in her bedroom mirror. The vacant look in her eyes actually scared her.

My gosh, she thought. I look too much like my own astral drop!

Cornelia shook herself. I've got to pull myself together, she decided. I've got to move on. Get over him.

She didn't know exactly how she was going to accomplish that feat. She took a long, cleansing breath, and some words of wisdom came to her mind. When she was no more than her sister Lilian's age, her dad had told her: "Getting from one place to another might seem hard, Cornelia, but it doesn't have to be. Just keep putting one foot in front of the other. Take step after step after step, and pretty soon you're far away from where you started."

Okay, she thought. So, that sounds really simpleminded and silly, but . . . One step: I'll get dressed. Another step: I'll get breakfast. A third step: I'll get to school.

And when I get there, she thought, I guess I'll figure out what the next step is!

Later that morning, the next step turned out to be something Cornelia never would have guessed.

Will showed up looking a total mess—as if she'd had a really bad night's sleep. That really disturbed Cornelia. The last time Will had looked like that, Nerissa had been giving her nightmares, keeping her up till all hours of the night.

During a break between classes, the girls met up in the hall and Will filled them in. Cornelia couldn't believe what had happened to Will; she'd experienced another nightmare all right, but it had happened when she was awake! And it had had nothing to do with Nerissa . . . it was her mother!

Will asked the other Guardians whether their astral drops had disappeared early, too. But theirs hadn't. Not one of the Guardians had experienced an astral-drop problem. Cornelia, Taranee, Hay Lin, and Irma had come home and reintegrated just fine with each of their astral drops.

"Nothing happened," Irma told Will.

"I can't believe it!" Will cried. "What do you mean, 'nothing happened'?"

"I mean just what I said," Irma replied. "Nothing happened!"

Taranee nodded. "Our astral drops were all in their places."

"It's true," Hay Lin added. "We reintegrated, and nobody noticed a thing."

Cornelia hated to see Will looking so defeated. And she hated to point out the obvious, but the conclusion was really clear. "Face the facts, Will," she said gently. "Your astral drop ran away from home."

Will rubbed her forehead. "What a disaster!

Do you realize what this means?" She turned away from her friends and began to pace, tapping her chin in agitation. "Somewhere out there is a person who's identical to me, talks like me, and has a part of my memories. Somebody who's *not* me!"

Cornelia glanced at the other Guardians. Were they thinking the same thing she was? Had Will's attitude toward her astral drop caused the problem? Will had never been very comfortable with the whole astral-drop thing. The first time she'd attempted to create Astral Will, she'd really messed up.

Back then, the real Will had been totally worried about creating a true double. She had feared that the girl would be so close to being an identical twin that she might actually steal her life.

So the astral girl Will created had known very little about Will's life—what to do, when to do it, who was who. To be safe, Will had had to write up a long note for her double to consult so she could even come close to capturing Will's behavior.

Even that hadn't worked. Astral Will had gotten confused her first morning in Will's apartment about whom to kiss before leaving for school. When Matt Olsen showed up at the door unexpectedly, Astral Will gave him the big kiss that should have gone to Will's mother!

And that wasn't the worst of it. After Astral Will realized she'd messed up, she'd tried to fix the situation. So when she'd seen Matt at school later that day, she'd hauled off and slapped him—right in the middle of the Sheffield courtyard!

Cornelia couldn't help raising an amused eyebrow at that memory. *Slapping Caleb,* she thought. Now *there's* an interesting idea for a new daydream!

"The craziest part is that I can't even go to the police to find her!" Will exclaimed.

"But you can always count on us," Taranee reminded her.

"Right!" Irma agreed.

Will stopped pacing and turned back to her friends. "What are you saying?"

"We'll split up and search Heatherfield," Irma told Will. "Your double can't have gotten very far."

Will hung her head. "But I can't help you. My mom grounded me."

"Even better," Cornelia quickly pointed out. "If your astral drop goes back home before we find her, you'll be there waiting for her!"

RIIIING!

"Okay, let's get to class, people!" called the vice-principal, striding down the hall. "The break's over!"

"It's agreed, then," Cornelia said, before they all headed off to their next classes. "We'll all meet outside the school, to launch Operation Recovery!"

A few hours later, the girls met up in the hall again. Everyone was geared up to get started on the search for Will's astral drop. Together, they walked toward the front gate of Sheffield.

"I like the name Operation Recovery," said Irma. "It sounds like something serious."

Taranee frowned. "Actually, Irma, this *is* something serious."

Cornelia rolled her eyes. Leave it to water girl to miss the boat, she thought, then noticed Will anxiously chewing her lip.

"Will, what's the matter?" Cornelia asked.

"I wish I could stick around and go with you all," she told the Guardians, "but I can't. Like I said before, my mom grounded me."

"Well," Irma cheerfully piped up, "you could replace yourself with *another* astral drop."

Everyone groaned.

"You're really with it today, Irma," Cornelia snapped. "Even smarter than usual."

Luckily, Will didn't seem bothered by Irma's suggestion. She gave her a small smile. "It's okay," she said. "And thanks for everything, guys."

The Guardians all nodded and smiled back at their leader. "No problem, Will," they replied in unison. "We've got your back. . . . Don't sweat it."

Suddenly, a sharp adult voice cut into the girls' tight circle. "Will!"

Cornelia looked up and saw Mrs. Vandom leaning against her parked car. Her arms were folded tightly across her chest, and her expression was grim.

"It's your mom," Cornelia quietly told Will. "Is she still angry? She looks it."

Will glanced over her shoulder and sighed heavily. "You should have seen her last night."

"Doesn't she even trust you to take the bus?" Irma whispered.

Will shook her head. "I can't believe she came to pick me up from school. I guess she's not done letting me have it."

"I'm sorry, Will," Cornelia whispered. "This isn't fair at all."

"Yeah," Will said, meeting Cornelia's eyes, "but then lots of things aren't fair lately, are they?"

Cornelia nodded, knowing exactly what Will meant. Caleb hadn't been fair to her when he broke her heart. But Cornelia wasn't going to let him break anything else in her life—not her spirit, not her determination, and certainly not her friendships!

Putting an arm around Will, Cornelia gave her a firm hug. "Don't worry," she said. "If your astral drop is out there, W.I.T.C.H. will find her."

"Will!" Mrs. Vandom called again.

"I better go," said Will.

"Us, too," said Cornelia, "'cause Operation Recovery is now officially under way!"

NINE

Will trudged toward her mother's car with all the enthusiasm of a condemned prisoner.

"About time," her mother snapped.

Will rolled her eyes. I *so* don't deserve to be treated like this, she thought.

She yanked open the passenger door while her mother walked around to the driver's side.

"Were you afraid I wouldn't go back home?" Will said after getting in and slamming the door. "Why did you have to wait for me outside the school? I'm not six years old anymore."

"Yeah?" her mother said as she started the engine. "It's a shame you behave as though you were!"

Will collapsed against the seat. Her mother had humiliated her in front of

her friends. But she was willing to forgive her
. . . *if* her mother would return the favor.

"Listen, Mom," Will said as politely as she
could. "I just wanted to tell you that—"

"Don't strain yourself," her mother replied,
steering the car out of the parking lot. "There's
no use trying to straighten things out."

Will squeezed her eyes shut. I can't believe
she just said that. I can't believe she's not willing to make up!

For a long, silent minute, Will studied her
mother's profile, waiting for a sign that her
frosty armor might actually crack, at least
enough for her mom to see that she had feelings, that there was another side to the story,
too!

But her mother remained as stiff as a statue.
Her brown eyes continued squinting at the
road ahead. Her glossy lips stayed frozen in an
angry frown.

Will sighed and gave up. She reached
around for the seat belt.

It just gets worse and worse, she thought.
Every day, every week that passes, everything
seems to get more difficult!

The car was quiet. Her mother didn't even

try to lighten her dour mood by turning on the radio. Out the window, trucks and buses rumbled by. On the sidewalk, pedestrians strode briskly along—businesspeople with briefcases, teenagers with backpacks. Children and grandparents, couples and single people, they all seemed sure of their destinations.

Point A to point B, Will thought. None of them probably even realize just how easy and *un*complicated their lives really are. She shook her head. They probably all think they've got it hard. They should try living a double life! Try being responsible for the safety of the universe. Try coming home after *saving* the universe, only to get grounded!

Sometimes Will wished she could turn back time and have her life be simple again. But then . . . it never really had been. Even when she'd *thought* she was living a normal life, she hadn't been!

Back before she and her mother had moved to Heatherfield, Will had lived in the small town of Fadden Hills. She'd gone to school, had babysitters, friendly teachers, a swim coach. She had never thought that anything was strange about them. But recently, she and

Hay Lin had followed a mysterious clue to a place in Fadden Hills. It was called the Rising Star Foundation. And it harbored some shocking truths for Will about the people in her old life.

For years, two former Guardians had been running the foundation in Will's hometown. Kadma and Halinor had raised orphans there. After some of those orphans grew up, they used them to spy on Will. For years, these spies had been entering Will's life. They would watch over Will, guide her, and report back to Kadma and Halinor on her progress.

Will had been stunned to learn all that. *Nothing* around her had happened by chance. None of the people around her were who she thought they were—not her babysitters, not her teachers, not her neighbors! The shock really jolted Will and made her wonder what a normal life would have been like.

Gazing out the car window now, Will noticed a mother and daughter walking along. The girl was about four or five. The mother looked really happy, smiling down at her little girl, holding her hand tightly.

Mom and I used to be like that, Will

thought. We used to have so much fun together, going shopping or out for ice cream. When we took drives, I could always get her to join in singing some silly song with me.

Will sighed and glanced back at her mother's grim expression.

There certainly isn't going to be any singing on *this* drive, she thought. I can't even get my mom to join in a civil conversation! And that's what I need right now, someone I can talk to. But the only person I want—my own mom—doesn't want to talk to me anymore!

Without a word, her mom pulled up to their apartment building. Will popped open the door. She knew her mother wouldn't be coming in. Her workday wouldn't be over for a few more hours.

"There's food ready for you in the fridge, Will," her mother called.

Will turned to reply, but her mother was already pulling away from the curb. So she just stood there, watching the car speed off down the block.

Yeah, Will thought, thanks for the oh-so-pleasant ride home, Mom! With a sigh of defeat, she turned and headed inside. She went up to her apartment and unlocked the door.

"It's a good thing I still have my friends to talk to," she murmured, shutting the door behind her. "And Matt, too." She trudged through the silent apartment. "Sooner or later, I'll find a way to tell him the truth about my life."

Will had tried to do that once already. The night of Mrs. Rudolph's retirement party at school, she'd confided everything to Matt. She'd told him about her double life, about the Guardians, and about the Heart of Candracar that lived inside her. She'd even called the Heart into her palm to show him. And when he'd asked to hold it, she'd thought nothing of passing it to him.

But she soon realized that she hadn't actually given the Heart to Matt. Nerissa had ruined everything that night. The nasty hag had taken over Matt's body. So, when Will confessed everything about her secret life, it had really been Nerissa who'd heard it. And when Will had called up the Heart, she'd stupidly handed it over to the wickedest villain in the known worlds!

"Okay," she muttered to herself, "not one of my smarter moments . . ."

That night had been a *big* mess up. Nerissa had used the Heart's power to attack Candracar. But with the help of the former Keeper, Cassidy, Will had regained the power of the Heart again. And W.I.T.C.H. had finally defeated Nerissa.

A lot has happened to me over the past few months, Will thought, but my feelings for Matt are still the same. Suddenly, she stopped and thought that over.

No, she mused, my feelings aren't the same. They're even stronger. In a lot of ways, I need Matt more than ever.

From the first day she'd met Matt Olsen, Will had been head over heels in love with him. Not only was he the lead singer of Cobalt Blue, he was an animal lover who helped out in his grandfather's pet shop and more importantly, a sweet and thoughtful friend.

"Someday, I'll reveal everything to him," she murmured, continuing to walk through the apartment. Will went to her bedroom and dropped her backpack on the floor. She noticed her little dormouse resting on the bedcovers.

"I totally love Matt," she told her dormouse. "And it's not supposed to be healthy for people in love to have secrets between them!"

Suddenly Will stopped and considered what she'd just said. *No secrets between people who love each other* . . . Cornelia used to think that, too, she realized. But look what happened once she revealed her true self to Caleb!

Oh, no! No, no, no! Will told herself. It's not the same. It's not the same at all! Matt didn't start out as a flower on another world. He's not a rebel leader with all sorts of . . . of *issues*. He's not that complicated. He's just a guy from Heatherfield!

Will paced back and forth. The dormouse watched her. Its little head swung one way, then another.

"Okay," Will whispered, "so Matt hasn't exactly said the words *I love you* to me yet. I know he mainly thinks of me as a good friend. But I'm sure he'll say those words someday!"

Will walked over to her cell phone. Maybe Matt's left a text message, she thought. Her heart sank when she remembered that her mother had taken the chip from inside the phone. Now she wouldn't even know whether Matt was trying to get in touch with her.

I'll call him in a few hours, she decided.

She didn't want to be so desperate. It was just that she missed him . . . a lot.

"Matt, Matt, Matt . . ." she quietly chanted, wishing she could conjure him up by reciting his name.

Well, she couldn't. But she *could* look at him. That would definitely make her feel better!

She walked over to her desk and opened a drawer. Lifting a pile of envelopes with one hand, she reached for her stack of snapshots with the other—

"My photos of Matt!" she cried. "Where are they?"

She looked closer. She dug around. Then she completely emptied the drawer. This was exactly where she'd last put photos of Matt she had taken over time. They were candids of the two of them and a few of just him. And now they were missing!

Will was hit by a dark thought. Could her mother have gone through her drawers and taken such meaningful keepsakes?

"She couldn't have taken them from me," she murmured. "She didn't even know they were there. . . . I'm the only one who knew about these photos. . . ."

That was when Will realized she was wrong. Someone else knew about those photos, too.

"It must've been my astral drop!" she cried. "But *why*? Why in the world would my astral drop steal my photos and run away?"

Will had a nagging feeling about it all. She glanced across the room. Her cell phone was still sitting on the edge of her bookshelf. She looked at it wondering what conversations it might have heard during her absence.

Not having it turned on was horrible! Because now, more than ever, she had to find her astral drop!

TEN

When Irma pushed open the door to the diner, she saw that the place was very crowded.

Another typical day at the Golden, she thought. She scanned all the tables filled with customers. Not one of the people looked like Will.

Irma split up from Taranee and Cornelia to cover the restaurant quickly. While they checked the restroom, she questioned people at the booths and tables. As the daughter of a police officer, she felt especially qualified to conduct the questioning. Unfortunately, none of the customers gave up any leads.

"Nothing!" Cornelia cried, throwing up her hands as they finally marched out of the diner. "Nobody's seen her here, either!"

No *duh*, Irma thought. Leave it to Corny to state the obvious.

"I say we're wasting time," Irma declared. "Her double could be anywhere. Why would her astral drop hang out at the same places Will does?"

"Because, Irma, it has the same memories as Will," Cornelia replied. "That's why!"

"How clever." Irma rolled her eyes. "I'm always amazed when I glimpse a bit of gray matter behind all that blond hair."

"You should try growing some yourself," Cornelia snapped back. "That way, you might start making more sense when you talk!"

Taranee laughed at that one, but Irma just folded her arms and shook her head. She was willing to cut Cornelia some slack because of Caleb. But just because Cornelia was heartbroken it didn't mean that she had to agree with her. So far, Cornelia's plan for finding Will's astral drop had been a bust.

Irma doubted that Astral Will would be hanging out at any of the places the real Will liked to go. The reason? Astral Will had run *away* from the real Will. So why would she risk running *into* her now?

Irma wished that she had a clue as to why Will's astral drop had run away. Something major must have happened. Irma tried to think like a detective. She knew the clues were there. . . . It was just a matter of knowing where to find them!

She knew that Will was very upset. Having a double of oneself running around unchecked is a bit freaky. Not too long ago her own astral drop had acted out of line. She'd come home after a W.I.T.C.H. mission to discover that Astral Irma had accepted a date with Martin Tubbs! And he was not exactly the dreamboat of Sheffield Institute.

Irma still shuddered at that memory. Thanks to her mother's insistence, she'd had to go through with the date.

Goofy, awkward, and skinny, with pants too short and large thick glasses, Martin had never—not in Irma's *weirdest* dreams—been boyfriend material. Of course, that hadn't stopped Nerd Boy from maintaining an annoying, puppy-dog crush on her.

Every time Martin saw her, he'd waggle his

sandy blond eyebrows and coo, "Sweet thing."

Totally gross, Irma thought. Luckily, he got the hint and stopped salivating by my locker. If he hadn't, I might have had to drop him in a lake!

Martin and Irma were actually friends now. But that was all—nothing more. Dating Martin Tubbs or any boy like him was not something Irma would ever do again! Not in her lifetime anyway, she thought. Which meant that the next time Astral Irma made a date with a lovesick geek, *she* was going to be the one to go out with him!

"Let's keep going, guys," said Cornelia, waving them down the street. "And keep your eyes open."

Irma draped an arm around Taranee's shoulder. "And as soon as you sense something, just whistle!"

She knew Taranee's psychic ability was sure to come in handy on that particular hunt!

"Don't worry," Taranee assured Irma. "All of my mental powers are in action. If that astral drop is in the area, you'll be the first to know."

The girls headed down the sidewalk. They passed a small city square with benches and tall trees. Up ahead was a shopping area.

"Have you guys heard any news from Hay Lin?" Cornelia asked.

"She said she'd catch up with us one way or the other," Irma informed them. "The little lady had an engagement she couldn't miss."

Taranee frowned. "And she didn't explain?"

"Nope," said Irma. "A total mystery. But she'd better have a great excuse for not being here."

Cornelia shrugged. "Her powers would have come in handy, but I think we can do it on our own."

As the girls moved down the street, Irma stole a glance at Cornelia. She was striding along with her shoulders squared and her chin high. She'd pulled all of her blond hair up into a no-nonsense ponytail. And with each brisk, determined step she took, her ponytail swung with bouncy energy.

Wow, Irma thought, Cornelia looks so together. There isn't one sign of tears or pain on her face. She's acting like she's already forgotten what happened with Caleb. . . .

But Irma found that hard to believe.

If Caleb were my boyfriend and he did that

to me, she thought, I'd want to stay under my bedcovers for weeks!

"Okay," Cornelia announced, coming to an abrupt stop on the sidewalk. "We're there."

Where? Irma wondered. This was a big, crowded city block. And Cornelia hadn't told them where their next stop would be. She'd just led the way.

"It's Matt's grandfather's pet shop," Taranee said, pointing to the little store on the corner.

Cornelia nodded. "It's another one of the addresses on our list. Will helps out here a couple afternoons a week. So it makes sense to check it out, don't you think?"

Irma laughed. "That's just an expression, right, Cornelia? I mean, you really don't care what I think, do you?"

Cornelia laughed. "Come on, let's go inside."

The girls pushed through the glass door. A little bell announced their arrival. The shop was adorable, clean, and cheerful, with shelves stocked with pet food and supplies. There were fish tanks full of sea creatures, golden cages holding colorful birds, and a few puppies and kittens waiting to be adopted.

Irma didn't waste any time. She barreled right up to the counter. Behind it stood Matt's grandfather, a little old man with wire-rimmed glasses. He wore a blue apron and a warm smile.

Mr. Olsen was a true animal lover. He sold pets to people only if he liked them and knew they'd give the animals good homes.

"Hello, Mr. Olsen," Irma said.

Beside the counter, a big blue parrot was perched on an open stand. *"Hello!"* it squawked.

The girls laughed, and so did Mr. Olsen. "Hi, there, girls," he said. "To what do I owe this surprise?" He glanced at Cornelia. "Problems with Napoleon?"

Cornelia stepped up to the counter. "No, it's not about my cat. To tell you the truth, we wanted to ask you about Will."

"Will!" he replied. "Maybe it's *you* who can tell *me* something about her. Is she having problems?"

Problems? What was he talking about? Irma wondered. She shared a confused glance with Cornelia and Taranee.

"Naturally, she doesn't tell me many

secrets," Mr. Olsen went on. "But you don't need to have eagle eyes to see that something's wrong. Yesterday she stopped by six times!"

Omigosh, Irma thought. He's talking about Astral Will! He has to be!

"What about today?" Irma quickly asked. "Has she come by yet?"

Mr. Olsen nodded. "That's the funny thing. I thought I saw her wandering around outside a couple times this morning. But she never came into the shop."

Irma's eyes grew wide—along with Cornelia's and Taranee's.

We've got her now, thought Irma. Or, at least, we've almost got her.

"I tried to talk to her," said Mr. Olsen. "But she ran off without saying a word."

Oh, no, Irma thought. I knew it sounded too good to be true.

Cornelia wasn't giving up easily. She drummed her fingers on the counter and looked at Matt's grandfather. "Well, when was the last time you saw her?"

He spread out his hands. "Less than an hour ago." Then he shook his head. "Honestly, I don't understand—"

Just then, Taranee interrupted. "I feel something . . . a presence!" She closed her eyes and put two fingers to her temples.

Mr. Olsen looked alarmed. Irma instantly jumped between him and Taranee. The last thing they needed just then was for Mr. Olsen to start getting curious about their powers.

"Did something happen to Will?" he asked.

"Uh, that's a really good question," Irma replied, stalling Matt's grandfather as Cornelia spirited Taranee away from the front counter. "But would you mind asking another one?"

Mr. Olsen shook his head in confusion. "Excuse me?"

"The astral drop," Taranee whispered, still concentrating with closed eyes. "I can feel her presence. . . ." Suddenly Taranee's head came up, and her eyes snapped open. "She's here!"

Cornelia could see that Astral Will wasn't in the store. So she rushed out to the sidewalk. Irma and Taranee hurried after her.

"I see her!" Cornelia cried, pointing across the street. "She's behind that tree!"

"What's going on, girls?" Mr. Olsen asked, stepping out of his shop. "Did you find Will?"

"It's okay, Mr. Olsen," Irma quickly said.

"We see her. Now we've got to hurry to catch up with her. Thanks! You've been very kind."

Irma was thrilled. Operation Recovery had worked! The only snag was that the second Matt's grandfather went back inside his shop, Astral Will took off!

"She must have seen us," Taranee said.

"Let's get her!" Irma cried.

The chase was on.

ELEVEN

Astral Will bolted from her hiding place behind the big tree.

They're looking for me, she realized. They want to stop me!

All day she'd been waiting for Matt to show up at his grandfather's store. But he hadn't come by. And now Will's friends were there! Astral Will had seen them go into the pet shop. And when they'd come out again, they'd pointed right at her!

Astral Will knew what they wanted. They wanted to drag her back to the real Will. They wanted her to reintegrate, to disappear again!

But Astral Will didn't want to disappear yet.

So she ran.

"Stop!" Irma cried.

Astral Will dropped her head and pumped her legs even harder. The city sidewalks were crowded. It made her getaway difficult. She dodged people like crazy, going left, then right, then left again.

The girls were closing in behind her. She could hear them on her heels.

"Man, is she fast!" Irma exclaimed behind her. "Can I make her slip in a puddle?"

"Are you crazy?" Cornelia cried. "No magic in public, Irma!"

Astral Will kept pumping with her legs and arms. I have to lose them, she thought. I have to get off this sidewalk!

She saw an alley ahead and ran into it, hoping to find a way to escape from the Guardians.

"They won't catch me! They won't catch me! They won't catch me!" she chanted.

But taking the alley was a mistake.

At the end of the long, shadowy passage, she saw a new street. But she couldn't get to it! A tall, locked gate blocked the way.

I messed up, she thought. I turned down a dead end. Now I'm trapped!

And her pursuers knew it, too.

"You're cornered, baby!" Irma shouted. She was breathing hard as she pounded the pavement right up to the trapped double. "This is the end of the line."

Cornelia and Taranee were right by her side.

"Don't be afraid of us," Cornelia called. "We don't want to hurt you."

"You're liars!" Astral Will spat.

If I can't get *through* this stupid gate, she thought, I'll get *over* it!

She grabbed on to the bars and pulled herself up. Her feet flailed, as she tried to get her footing. Once she did, she'd boost herself right over the top and escape!

"Quick!" Cornelia shouted to the other girls. "Don't let her get away!"

Taranee, Irma, and Cornelia all jumped at the same time. They grabbed the double's coat and pulled.

"*Arrrgh!*" Astral Will cried, straining against them. She held on to the bars with all of her might. *I'm not letting go!* she promised herself. *I'm not letting them stop me!*

"Ugh!" Cornelia groaned, struggling to yank Will's double free of the gate. "She's stronger than she looks."

"Aaagh!" Taranee wailed, losing her grip.

"Get down from there!" Irma shouted. "Let go!"

Will's friends pulled harder. Then, suddenly—

Rrriiiippp!

Irma accidentally tore Astral Will's coat. Dozens of photos spilled out of her pocket and fluttered down to the pavement.

Astral Will glanced over her shoulder. She saw Irma drop to the ground and begin picking up the photos.

"These are photos of Matt!" Irma cried in surprise.

"Don't touch them!" Astral Will shrieked. She let go of the gate and dropped down. Then she wound up her arm and—

SLAP!

Irma reeled. The photos flew out of her hand.

"Don't touch them!" Astral Will shrieked again, ready to launch herself at Irma once more.

Cornelia and Taranee leaped forward and pulled Will's double back.

"Let me go! Let me go!" Astral Will yelled as

she struggled against them. But Will's friends were too strong. She couldn't break away. They were flanking her now, each girl tightly holding one of her arms.

Astral Will glared at Cornelia, but she couldn't do anything more. They held her in a tight grip.

"Take it easy!" Cornelia warned. "Take it easy!"

Taranee's eyes were wide behind her round glasses. And Irma stood gaping in shock at Will's double, as if staring at a girl who'd gone totally crazy.

I don't care what anyone thinks, Astral Will told herself. I know exactly what I'm doing. And I know why I'm doing it!

Taranee turned her head toward Irma. "Are you okay, Irma?" she asked.

Irma rubbed her reddening cheek. "Yeah . . . I'm fine."

"Let me go!" Astral Will demanded again, struggling against the Guardians' grip. "Please! Don't take me back to her!"

"To who?" Taranee asked.

"To Will!" cried the astral drop. "Don't take me back to Will! I don't want to disappear again. I . . . I . . . I want to live!"

"Live! Don't be ridiculous!" Irma exploded. She'd recovered from her shock. Now she looked really angry. She stepped up to the struggling astral drop and shook a finger in her face. "You're just an astral drop!"

"That's not true," Astral Will spat back. "I breathe! I think! I have feelings, just like you do!"

Will's friends fell silent for a minute, as if they didn't know what to say. *Good*, thought Astral Will. They've stopped yelling. Maybe they're ready to listen.

"If I go back to Will, she'll make me disappear forever," said the astral drop, "and I . . . I'll never see *him* again."

Why is it so hard to explain things? she thought. Why is it so hard to try to make people understand? All of a sudden, she felt her internal energy crashing. She stopped struggling against Cornelia and Taranee. And she fell, limp, in the girls' arms. Tears welled up in her eyes.

Taranee and Cornelia released their grip on her. She slumped backward against the gate. The tears were now pouring out.

"Who's she talking about?" Taranee whispered.

"I'm talking about the boy I love!" Astral Will told them. "Matt Olsen."

"What?" Cornelia cried.

Astral Will nodded. "Ever since that time he kissed me, I haven't been able to stop thinking about him. . . ."

How many times have I relived that sweet, sweet kiss? she asked herself. A hundred? A thousand? In her mind, she remembered it all so clearly.

It had happened that first morning—when she woke up in Will's bedroom. She remembered how everything had felt . . . so new and strange, so scary and . . . *wonderful*!

She remembered the funny feeling of brushing her teeth for the first time—the odd squishiness of the toothpaste tube. She remembered the delicious smell and taste of the warm croissant.

And she remembered kissing Matt Olsen.

He had come to the door that morning to deliver Will's little dormouse back to her. And he had looked so cute, with his shaggy brown hair and big warm eyes. He'd worn baggy jeans and an easygoing smile that lit up the room.

She remembered his babbling something about not being able to watch Will's dormouse another night. It had kept his parents up or something.

That was when it had happened. The original Will had given her a list of things to do while W.I.T.C.H. was away on their mission. But Astral Will hadn't had the list in her hand when she answered the door.

She'd known she was supposed to kiss someone good-bye. She just hadn't realized it was Will's *mom*. So instead, she'd kissed Matt!

She still remembered it all vividly. She'd stepped forward and put her hands on Matt's shoulders. She had pulled him toward her and pressed her lips to his. His mouth was warm. And the scraggly whiskers on his chin tickled her face.

She remembered Matt's eyes going wide and googly. Then his arms had fallen to his sides. He had really liked the kiss; she could see that!

And she remembered how much she had enjoyed the kiss, too. That was the boy Will liked. And Astral Will had all of Will's feelings.

She would always remember that flip-floppy feeling going through her—like a singing, pulsing electrical current!

Her first experience taking Will's place had been confusing, but exhilarating. And now, given another opportunity to live Will's life, Astral Will found that her emotions were even more intense than before. Her feelings for Matt had become overwhelming. And she just couldn't bear the idea of being ripped away from him once again!

Especially now, she thought. Things have taken such a terrible turn. I just couldn't stand to leave knowing that . . .

"He's betrayed me," she confessed to Will's friends.

"What?" said Irma. "Matt's betrayed you? How?"

Astral Will hung her head. "I hate Matt now," she declared. "But . . . at the same time, I can't live without him!"

Feeling totally lost, she raised her head. More tears slipped from her eyes. "If you can understand what I feel, help me!" she wailed. "I'm so unhappy!"

Will's friends glanced at one another. They looked concerned but confused.

"Just let me go," Astral Will pleaded. "I'll talk with Matt one last time, and then I'll disappear forever. I promise!"

TWELVE

As identical as two drops of water, Taranee thought, shaking her head. That's what an astral drop was supposed to be—a tangible, thinking double.

An astral drop wasn't supposed to run away and demand a life separate from the Guardian who had conjured her up! She was supposed to fill in for a Guardian without raising suspicions among family and friends. She was supposed to be a faithful, obedient being!

At least that was what Taranee had thought . . . until now.

Will's astral drop wasn't behaving anything like the Will that Taranee knew. She was acting way too emotional. She seemed totally panicked and frantic.

Plus, she was freaking about Matt's "betraying" her. What in the heck was the girl talking about? Taranee wondered. I've never heard of any "betraying."

"This is crazy," she told the other Guardians. "An astral drop who's in love? There wasn't anything about this in the script!"

Cornelia shook her head. "But that's how it is, Taranee—"

"Stop!" Irma warned Cornelia. "If you're about to say something about the 'uncontrollable power of love,' save it! We've got a problem here of tragic proportions!"

Oh, man, thought Taranee. The water Guardian's running mouth strikes again. I mean, after everything Cornelia's been through, how could Irma *say* that!

She waited for Cornelia to rip into Irma. But Cornelia didn't. She remained cool, calm, and collected. Ignoring Irma, she simply turned to Astral Will and said, "There's something I still don't understand. What exactly happened between you and Matt?"

Astral Will's head was down. Her bright red hair was hanging in her eyes. "Yesterday," she said, slowly lifting her head. "It happened yesterday. He invited me out for a long bike ride."

The astral drop's expression became glassy-eyed and dreamy. "We hung out and talked . . . all afternoon. . . ."

Whoa, Taranee told herself, this girl has really got it bad for Matt!

Suddenly, Taranee stopped and considered what she'd just observed. Uh-oh, she thought, does that mean the real Will feels this way, too? I mean, I know Will really likes Matt and everything . . . but I never saw her completely lose her mind over the guy.

"Go on," Cornelia gently coaxed Astral Will, interrupting Taranee's thoughts.

"I couldn't find the courage to tell him what I really felt for him," said the astral drop. "I said good-bye without telling him how much that kiss meant to me, even if it did happen by accident!"

"So, you ran away from home to tell him that?" Irma guessed.

Astral Will nodded vigorously. "I tried calling him, but it was useless! He wasn't answering his phone. So I sneaked out. I know I shouldn't have done it."

Irma narrowed her eyes. "Will paid dearly for your little stroke of genius," she snapped. "She's in big trouble now, thanks to you!"

Astral Will's eyes began to tear up again. "I know," she said, "and I'm really, really sorry . . . but I had to talk to Matt."

"So, what happened?" Cornelia pressed.

"I walked around the city for hours," Astral Will replied. "He was busy rehearsing with his band. And he still wasn't answering his phone. So I caught up with him in person. I wanted to surprise him, and . . ." The astral drop's voice trailed off. She hugged herself and studied her thick-soled shoes.

"And?" said Irma. "And what?"

"And I saw it all," said the astral drop.

"What did you see?" Irma pressed.

"He was with a *girl*!" she wailed, tears springing to her eyes again. "And he had her in his arms!"

Taranee felt her stomach drop. She glanced at Irma—whose mouth was hanging open. Cornelia had grown pale; in fact, she looked completely shocked. Taranee was sure that Cornelia could completely understand the feelings of hurt and rage coursing through Astral Will.

What is this, anyway? thought Taranee, *Betray a Guardian Week?*

In Taranee's view, this was even worse than what had happened between Cornelia and Caleb. Will had been seeing Matt on a regular basis. He didn't live in another world. He wasn't trying to save Candracar or be a Metamoorian rebel. They went out on dates. They talked on the phone and sent text messages. Matt was human!

Just like me and Nigel, thought Taranee, glancing at the other Guardians.

So what now? she wondered. Will had looked superstressed at school that day. Hearing this news wasn't going to make things easier for her.

Everyone fell silent for a long time. Taranee assumed they were all wondering the same thing she was: how are we going to break this news to Will? The *real* Will?

With a sigh, Cornelia took Astral Will by the arm. She gently guided her out of the alley. Taranee and Irma followed. The girls crossed the street to a small park and collapsed on the nearest bench.

"So, what do we do?" Taranee finally asked.

Irma sighed. "Maybe there's someone else who should know about all this, don't you think?"

"Of course," Taranee replied. "Did you want to tell her yourself?"

"Not on your life!" Irma shook her head. She got quiet for a few seconds—as if she were thinking it over. Then she pointed at Astral Will. "*She's* going to tell her."

"Me?" cried the astral drop.

"Yeah, you," Irma said.

Taranee chewed on her lip. Will's double looked positively miserable. And Taranee hated to see Astral Will made even more miserable than she already was. However, Irma's idea made sense.

After all, thought Taranee, Astral Will is the one who actually saw Matt with another girl. So, of course, she should be the one who should tell Will about it.

Come to think of it, Taranee realized, if I had to hear bad news about Nigel, my astral drop would probably be the best one to hear it from. I mean, how can you not believe words that come out of your own mouth?

Wait a second, Taranee silently told herself.

It's not really your own mouth. Not until you reintegrate with it . . .

Aargh! she thought. This whole thing is just too complicated! She massaged her temples. And it's giving me a headache!

The girls sat in silence for another long minute.

At last, Astral Will spoke up. "This means you're not going to let me go, right?" she asked dejectedly.

Cornelia put a hand on the double's shoulder. "We can't, Will . . ." Then she smiled at the girl. "Can I call you Will?"

For the first time since they had caught her, Astral Will smiled.

THIRTEEN

"So . . . who was that girl?" Will asked her astral drop. She couldn't believe the story that she was hearing from her double's lips!

"I don't know," said Astral Will. "I never saw her before!" The astral drop sat on Will's bed. Her head was in her hands. Cornelia, Taranee, and Irma were hanging out on the fringes. Cornelia stood in one corner. Irma stood in another, while Taranee was slumped in Will's desk chair. None of the Guardians had said a word since the astral drop started talking. Nobody knew what to say.

Will sighed. She stood at her bedroom window. The sun was just setting over Heatherfield, creating a beautiful landscape of color. Normally Will loved looking at the sunset, but tonight she wasn't focusing on the sky. She was having trouble focusing on anything at the moment. Her mind was reeling from everything she'd just learned from her double.

Fifteen minutes ago, Cornelia, Taranee, and Irma had knocked on her front door. They'd found Astral Will and brought her back home.

That was the good news.

The bad news had come from her astral drop. She claimed she'd seen some girl in Matt's arms.

"I'm sorry, Will!" cried the double.

"No," said Will. She turned from the window and went to her astral drop. "I'm the one who's sorry . . . for you." She sat on the bed and put a hand on Astral Will's slender shoulder.

"That kiss . . . the pictures," said Will, "and those phone calls to Matt. I found them listed on my cell phone, you know."

Astral Will groaned and shook her head. "I was trying to call him, but he wasn't answering. So I went to find him . . . and . . ."

"I know," said Will. "You told me everything. What I'm trying to say is . . ." She shook her head. "You didn't deserve this. Neither of us deserved it. But maybe it's best that it all turned out this way. After all, to Matt, I'm just a good friend."

Will closed her eyes a moment and took a deep breath. It was hard to admit it, but she couldn't come to any other conclusion. Matt had never said he loved her. Sure, she'd wanted him to, but he'd never actually come out and said it.

If what her astral drop was saying was true, Matt was obviously interested in some other girl. The astral drop claimed she had seen the two with her own eyes and that her heart had been shredded because of it.

"I thought a reflected image couldn't suffer," Will told her double, "but I was wrong. And I'm sorry you had to go through all of this."

Astral Will stood up. She wiped the tears from her cheeks. "The thing that hurts the most," she confessed, "is knowing that I'm just a reflection."

On the floor nearby, Will's dormouse made a squeaking sound. He emerged from underneath the bed and turned his furry little face up to stare at Astral Will. He blinked in confusion for a moment. And then he swung his head to stare at the real Will.

Back and forth the creature's little head went. Desperately, he tried to figure out why there were two Wills! Finally, he gave up. With a final, confused squeak, he ran back under the bed.

Will stood up to face her astral drop. Sometimes she felt like her dormouse—totally disturbed by the entire astral-drop thing. She suspected all of the Guardians had the same nagging feelings about their doubles. But for some reason, she always ended up the most freaked out about the drops.

Conversing with an astral drop was like talking to a three-dimensional mirror image of yourself that could actually talk back!

It wasn't easy for Will to come face to face with the imperfections in herself. She found herself way too flat-chested and gawky. Her lips were too thin, and some of her expressions looked downright goofy.

And the really freaky thing is that this isn't some other person who just *looks* like me, Will thought, this *is* me.

But that wasn't what disturbed Will the

most. She had never liked the idea that Astral Will could take her place.

What girl wants to believe that she could be replaced? she thought.

At least my very best friends aren't fooled by Astral Will, she thought. But my mother and Matt *were* easily fooled. So what does that say about my relationships with them?

Ugh, she thought, why even think like that? She suddenly had another thought and looked over at the saddened astral drop.

"Where does an astral drop go when she's not here?" Will asked her double.

The astral drop thought for a moment. Then she shook her head. "I can't say, Will. It's a kind of elsewhere that might not even exist. Someplace inside of you, maybe."

"Inside of me?" said Will.

"I mean . . ." the astral drop shrugged. "Maybe I'm just one of your dreams."

Will put a hand on her double's shoulder. "Maybe," she said, "but, you know, I think it's time for us to join back together now."

Astral Will's body tensed. Her hands formed fists, and her eyes went from frightened to serious. She frowned at Will.

"My memories are going to become yours," she warned. "You won't like them this time."

Will knew that. But she wasn't going to run away from them. She knew that running away would not solve anything.

Suddenly, she froze. Wait a second, she said to herself. Could *that* be the part of me that can't be copied? The part that doesn't run away? The part that's not afraid to stand and fight?

Deep inside, Will knew the answer. And her spirits lifted. Because Will Vandom finally realized that she couldn't be copied—not totally. There would always be a part of her that was truly special, the part that made her the Keeper of the Heart.

And Will knew that the same was true for all of the Guardians. Just look at Cornelia, she thought. Caleb dumped her, but she didn't run away. She didn't hide under the bedcovers all day. She found her inner strength. She came to school. She faced her friends. She went on with her life. She even led the way in tracking down my lost astral drop!

Will doubted whether Cornelia's own astral drop could have done all that. No . . . there was something inside each of the Guardians that made them unique and special, that made them W.I.T.C.H.!

With renewed courage, Will turned to stand directly in front of her astral drop. "I'm ready," she said.

Without a sound, the astral drop closed her eyes and stepped toward Will. Light swirled around them as they came together, and the two became one again.

Will felt the currents of energy whirling around her. A small part of herself had returned. An empty pocket deep inside was being filled again.

That was when the memories began flooding into her. Images entered her mind like bits of information downloading into a computer.

The surge of pictures was confusing at first. Everything was out of order. She saw Olsen's Pet Shop and Sheffield's classrooms. She saw herself riding her bicycle and heard her mother talking about her day at work. There were flashes of color and random bits of dialogue.

Will recognized her bedroom and her dormouse. Then she saw her best friends chasing her down a narrow alley. She saw a gate blocking her escape. Saw herself striking Irma—

"Oh, gosh," she whispered. "Sorry, Irma."

She felt herself struggling. Cornelia and Taranee were holding her tight. Then, suddenly, time jumped backward.

She saw the night before. There was a long, desperate walk around the city. It was cold. And she felt alone and scared, confused and angry. . . .

Olsen's Pet Shop appeared again. And there was Mr. Olsen. Then came the park, and the pet shop, *again*. Obviously, she'd been hanging around the shop all day, waiting for Matt to show.

"Matt . . ." Will murmured.

Finally, Will saw him.

It was suddenly the afternoon of the previous day. Will and Matt were riding bikes together and talking. The weather was beautiful. He was beautiful, too . . . with his shaggy brown hair and brown eyes.

Will saw herself laughing at his bad jokes. She sighed over his carefree, laid-back attitude. He brushed her bangs away from her face. And she smiled up at him. It was all so perfect.

Then the scene changed.

Will saw the cell phone in her hand. She was

making call after call to Matt. He never picked up. She felt the urgency to see him, and saw herself leaving the apartment to look for him.

And then she found him.

His shaggy brown hair, his handsome face, his big brown eyes. And his strong arms, wrapped tightly around . . .

"No . . ." Will rasped.

She had known this was coming. Astral Will had warned her. But nothing could have prepared her for the sight itself.

Will didn't recognize the person in Matt's arms. The girl's face was hidden, turned toward Matt. But Will could see one thing. They were a pair. Now she could see exactly why Astral Will had been suffering so badly. . . .

The shattering pain of Matt's betrayal was almost too much to bear. She understood why her astral drop had run away.

Will closed her eyes as all the memories flooded into her mind. She focused on the power inside her, her inner core that could never be replicated. Then she turned to look at her friends.

I need my friends now, she thought. They understand. Heartache is painful, and to be surrounded by good friends makes all the difference in the world. Yes, I may have just had my heart broken, but the Power of Five is stronger than ever. And that means, I can get through anything . . . including this.